Peter

HIDDEN AGENDAS

Inside Town Hall

A Novel

FRANK B. CONNOLLY

ISBN: 1539524248
ISBN 13: 9781539524243
Library of Congress Control Number: 2017908769
CreateSpace Independent Publishing Platform
North Charleston, South Carolina

IT'LL PASS . . . IT'LL PASS

"What. . . what . . ." Startled, Dominic's heart skipped a beat. He started to turn his head, but before he could turn his massive neck, a gloved hand harshly covered his gaping mouth.

"Shut up and just listen" the menacing male voice growled, sending shivers down Dominic's body. He began to shake uncontrollably under the cold grip of the unrelenting glove, suddenly regretting where he parked. There was no one else around.

The hand loosened its grip on his face and dropped to his bulging neck. "You know what happens if this project fails?"

"It'll pass . . . It'll pass." Dominic exclaimed hastily as he worked his jaw that was stiff from the grip of the glove. He instantly recognized the voice, Louie "The Enforcer."

He knew who the ominous person represented, and he knew the Enforcer's reputation! Dominic wiped the saliva from the corners of his mouth, tasting the leather from the intruder's glove. He swallowed hard several times. "I'm, . . I'm gonna take care of things. No shit. I'll make more calls to the Commissioners and. . . and . . . I'll remind them of a few things they want to forget – things they REALLY want to forget."

"Maybe it's you that people will want to forget," the voice said with a sneer.

Dominic shook again, shivers racking his massive frame. "I know things, nasty things. I . . . I can help sway their thinking."

Chapter 1
THE PUBLIC HEARING

Wednesday, February 27

"Order in the room! Order in the room!" shouted Jim Bradley as he struggled desperately not only to control the unruly crowd in the overheated jammed meeting room, but his own temper as well. His voice held more than a trace of exasperation as he boomed out over the catcalls, the booing and the hissing. Sweat dripped on his brow. His narrow face, normally reflecting a pleasant disposition, was glowing red with anger and fatigue; his knuckles were white from his tight grip on the oak gavel. His blood pressure, normally within the limits of a healthy fifty-year-old, would have provoked his doctor to immediately order a stress test. Fortunately, his doctor was not in the agitated angry crowd, having chosen to stay home enjoying a good novel rather than attend the local public meeting. Jim cast his stern gaze into the livid eyes glaring back at him. He did not flinch. He straightened his back with renewed intent. The bulging furrows of his forehead further underscored his intent to maintain control of the scene before him.

As Chairman of the Planning and Zoning Commission, Jim had the unenviable duty of running the Commission's public hearings and calling on the various speakers. Past experience had taught him the importance of controlling the tempo of the meeting, and tonight's meeting, the third consecutive night on the controversial shopping center proposal, was testing his years of experience - and his patience. His normal command of public meetings had given way to a determination to just regain control of the meeting tempo.

"Quiet. . . Quiet. . . " He slammed the gavel several times. Only its hard oak composition saved it from splintering into fragmented toothpicks. "Order, please! This meeting will be conducted in an orderly fashion. Pilgrim Enterprises has the right to finish its presentation on its shopping center proposal before this Commission without continual interruption. Attorney Cimione has the floor. Please allow him to finish his. . ."

"It's not their town!" bellowed an agitated man from the rear of the room.

"Yea, tell them to go home," a woman's voice shouted out to the glee of the residents in the room. Her outburst was greeted with another cascade of cheers, boos, and catcalls.

"We don't want their kind here," another voice boomed out.

"Tell'm where to stick their shopping center," a man in jeans with a short red beard yelled. The crowd again erupted, a feeling of blood spectator sport creeping in. The man slowly sat down and snickered, a wry grin on his face.

The gavel slammed down again. "Order! If this keeps up, I will adjourn this meeting," threatened Bradley. "Enough!"

After three hours of heated arguments between the developers and the agitated citizens, the room's atmosphere resembled the local gym's steam room: hot, stuffy, and a humidity level that made everyone's clothes cling to them, soggy, droopy and uncomfortable. The overcrowding of the school cafeteria made it even worse, adding to everyone's discomfort and attitude. Outside, the frigid Connecticut February air offered a sharp contrast to the sweltering room. A deep black night with a soft February snow falling. Silent. Cold. Peaceful. Very Peaceful. The soft snow blanketed the air, and muffled any sounds.

In the daytime, this meeting room, the cafeteria in Covingford's aging high school, was a pleasant place, a place of friendship, laughter, joviality and animated conversation. The names and photos of Covingford's winning school warriors hung on the soccer, football and basketball banners adorning the walls. But tonight, these silent warriors stared down not on a bubbling high school crowd, but rather, upon a crowd of enraged citizens. Tonight was not a night of recognition for these school heroes, nor of school affairs. No, tonight was a night of other warriors - of parents and neighbors who felt threatened and were ready to do battle. Their neighborhood was threatened, their way of life faced change, unacceptable change. Justice was demanded. If their town officials could, or would, not fight the developers, they would. This was their town. The war was starting.

———

Kurt Thomas, Town Manager of Covingford, scanned the room. He looked out on the angry crowd jammed into the aisles, packed against the walls, some even sitting against the frosted windowsills. Every entrance was filled. Fortunately the local Fire Marshal was not present to check the emergency access areas, nor to check on the posted limit of 175 people. Kurt knew that if the Marshal was present, his job would have been a difficult one, as he would have had to argue with the 250 people in the room, most of whom were in no mood to be told what to do. He would not have won. Perhaps by accident, but more likely by design, he was not there. *Just as well*, thought Kurt.

Kurt momentarily disregarded the churning throng of people to concentrate on the stout fat man standing in back. As usual, thought Kurt, the man's sloppy appearance with his stained shirt hanging out over his gigantic waist, was quite in keeping with his character. The poor lighting in that corner of the cafeteria shrouded the portly silhouette, but Kurt knew, unmistakably, that it was Dominic "the Bomb" Columbo, Chairman of the local political Town Committee. Kurt did not have to see the large man's face to know that Dominic was staring intensely back at him. He could sense the stare, feel the hatred. It flowed across the room, unmitigated in its intensity. Kurt steadily returned the stare.

"This project will only bring in more outsiders and ruin Covingford," guffawed an elderly lady who had been sitting quietly in the third row, her fingers deftly working her knitting. "Next thing you know they will be building a fast food joint." More cheering erupted in strong support of the knitter. They were behind her. She was the little 5'1" elderly widow from Cedar Street who greeted all her neighbors every day with a cheerful "good morning" and "good evening." Tonight they loved her even more, the quiet unassuming little old lady turned gladiator.

The crowd was fired up, reacting immediately to each catcall. Tonight, the third straight night of the public hearings on the proposed shopping center, had seen the mob turn ugly. The focus of their animosity, their enemy, was the developer of the proposal, Pilgrim Enterprises, represented by the president of the firm and an unlucky associate. These two people, the outsiders, posed the threat to Covingford's way of life: they were the child snatchers, the predators of widows, the sex offenders, the Wall Street tycoons, the Ponzi manipulators, the destroyers of pristine open space, the devil incarnate!

"Please. Let them finish," bellowed Bradley. "We can then conclude this hearing. It's getting late."

Kurt sensed the exasperation in the chairman's voice. It had been a long night for Bradley, and clearly, Kurt realized, he had reached his breaking point. Three consecutive nights of hearings, each more agitated than the previous, had brought the mild mannered Bradley to his limit. Kurt glanced around and spotted Janet Johnson, the newspaper reporter for the Hartford Inquirer. She was quite attractive in her neat black skirt, white blouse, and auburn hair pulled back and held in place by a silver barrette. She was just a few feet away, seated in the front row. *A picture of composure,* he thought, *a true newspaper reporter. She did not want to miss anything. Not a damn thing.* Kurt smiled inwardly as he realized that Bradley's troubles in controlling the heated meeting were Janet's bread and butter. "It's all here," he whispered to himself, "yes, the material reporters loved – conflict, excitement, angry citizens – newspaper heaven." He thought he even detected a smile on her face as she wrote feverishly in her notepad. Her dimples bounced in and out, almost in rhythm. *Yes, tonight's her night—and tomorrow's headlines will be the nightmare for the developer.*

The representatives of Pilgrim Enterprises, the project developers, sat quietly in the rear of the room. Despite efforts to blend with the audience, everyone in the room knew who they were. They were the outsiders, the destroyers of their town, the enemy. The developers tried to ignore the enmity. They had seen this reaction before at other local public meetings, had anticipated it, and prepared for it - or thought they did. The weeks of careful planning suddenly seemed for naught. They had hired Dick Cimione, the resident attorney who knew the ins and outs of the planning process. He frequently appeared before the Planning and Zoning

Commission on behalf of developers, and he was the local "go to" attorney. Cimione knew the Commissioners, their mannerisms, their likes and dislikes. He knew all about each Commissioner, their families, their occasional indiscretions. Few secrets stayed secret in small towns like Covingford. Local gossip, after all, helped pass away many a long winter's night.

The developers knew it was not wise to hire an unknown out-of-town attorney for this type of presentation, but rather to hire a "local." Knowledge of the local scene was as important, if not more so, than the strict letter of zoning law. Cimione, pushing 60, fit the bill. After all, he had been in law practice in Covingford for over 25 years. This had been the developer's game plan, carefully planned and carried out. He was their esteemed spokesman, their hired gun. But tonight, something was amiss. The plan was not working. And now, they watched warily as Attorney Cimione again approached the podium for his closing remarks.

Cimione hesitantly reached the podium and stood beside the perplexed chairman. Cimione deliberately looked out over the unruly crowd, his ruffled thinning hair drooping over his rotund sweaty face. He patiently waited for the noise in the room to quiet down. As the noise receded, Bradley turned to the attorney, and with a fleeting sense of relief, turned the podium over to him. He noticed the apprehensive look on Cimione's face as he stepped aside and quietly moved behind the attorney. His eyes focused on the balding circle on the back of Cimione's head. "Almost a monk's head" he mused to himself, "but certainly in appearance only."

Cimione stood quietly; he continued his scan of the room. He slowly gripped the podium with his strong hands if he was going to lift it up. The thought of throwing it at the crowd flashed briefly through his mind. He laughed inwardly. Loosening his tie and unbuttoning his top button, he wiped the beads of sweat off his forehead with his handkerchief. The salt burned his eyes. Sensing the decrease in the noise levels, he started in his best oratorical voice. "For the last three nights I have presented a clear and fair picture of this proposal and its benefits to Covingford. It will. . ."

"Go to hell!" a voice cried out.

". . . it will help the town," he continued, ignoring the interruption. "The shopping center will feature the well-known upscale grocery store chain Hoity-Toity as the center's anchor store. The entire proposal will occupy about 25 acres, and will contain several popular retail stores. Stores you will like, stores you will shop in, even a restaurant. This proposal will add more than 400 jobs. The developers are committed to hiring local residents first. And certainly it will add to Covingford's tax base. . ."

"And its traffic. . . " an enraged male voice shouted out.

"Hoity-Toity to the toitee," another citizen yelled out, followed by laughter and sneers.

Again ignoring the interruption and suppressing his irritation, Cimione struggled to continue. "Hoity-Toity is a well-established upscale grocery store that has other branches in the South and wants to make its debut here in Connecticut. It will be an asset to the town and a major addition." Turning to face the other four members of the PZC who were seated together at the table to his left, he continued in his practiced steady and somewhat confident voice, despite an inwardly sickening feeling that he was losing the battle. The Commissioners sat immobilized, returning his stare. Three men and one woman, who, with their Chairman Jim Bradley, constituted the five member PZC. At this time, they were the center point of Covingford, the PZC entrusted with making the decision of approving or disapproving the shopping center. They said nothing. Each one struggled to maintain an expressionless face so as not to indicate whether he or she was in favor of or against the proposal. The four of them and the Chairman were the judges. They were the impartial local authority of five, vested under Connecticut law of voting on zone changes. They had the responsibility of guiding Covingford's land use development.

"Commission members, ladies and gentlemen," Cimione continued, "I have previously introduced several experts who addressed the issues of traffic, air quality, environmental protection, erosion control, tax revenue, and economic improvement. Their testimony shows that there will be minimum impact on the neighborhood. We have proposed road improvements to address this impact. We are planning extensive landscaping, numerous tree plantings, waves of flowers - in effect a real picturesque showcase. When we finish, the area will be an asset to Covingford, not the overgrown look of a vacant lot full of weeds and woods that's out there now. Our proposal will dramatically increase the tax base, without a big demand on town services. Right now this parcel is generating nothing for Covingford, nothing, except collecting trash and litter. We want to make improvements; we want to clean up the area and change. . ."

"Boo . . . Boo . . . Go home!"

"Yea, get the hell outta here!"

The crowd reveled in the interruptions and vigorously clapped for each outburst to show their support. Janet continued to scribble notes for her news article without even looking up, a very broad smile on her petite face. *Better than any crime show on Wednesday night TV. These meetings make such great news.* She knew her editor would love the story - the fighting, the turmoil, the accusations, the personal attacks. She always marveled and wondered why there were not more libel lawsuits that came out of these hearings. Tonight's meeting would temporarily increase circulation, and if it's a really slow news day, even make the front page - a *good bonus.*

Blogs would fly, tweets would tweet. She continued to write, the words flowing like boiling lava. Words, she knew, when they hit the glare of the headlines in the morning, would have the same effect as boiling lava.

Bradley, sensing that the meeting was again getting out of control, moved to the podium and stood beside Cimione. He banged the gavel several times and the outcries decreased. He looked out over the packed room and absorbed the intense anger of the crowd. The other four PZC members continued to sit with frozen expression on their faces, glad, very glad, that their chairman and not themselves, was running the meeting. "Please" Bradley implored, "Mr. Cimione is almost finished."

"Damn right he's finished." More cheers, but at a lower decibel level.

Cimione stood erect, his beady bloodshot eyes squinted with sweat. He secretly thanked Jim for moving up to the podium beside him. It not only provided another target, but it gave him a moment to organize his thoughts and retrench his arguments. His dark blue suit hung on him like a sagging canvas tent after a summer thunderstorm, covering his soaked white shirt. The temperature in the overcrowded cafeteria, like the tempers of the infuriated citizens, had risen a few more degrees. It certainly would have been the ideal time for the Board of Education to request funding for central air conditioning for their aging facility, a move that would have passed unanimously, even by the senior citizens in the room.

Sensing a slight decrease in the noise level, Cimione took back the microphone and continued. "In closing, I say again, this proposal is good for Covingford. It will improve the area, increase the tax base, and provide local jobs. This property is on the market, and this is a good use." Turning slightly to make eye contact with the four PZC Commissioners on the stage, he continued. "On behalf of my clients, I am therefore requesting approval by you of our proposal." He paused, and stepped back momentarily from the podium. He wiped his brow with his handkerchief. His steady bleary eyes surveyed the room, his exterior demeanor calm, despite his inner feelings. He then faced the crowd, reached for the microphone, and continued in a slow but deliberative tone. "I live in this town too, and let me offer you this. Covingford is changing, it's growing. That's inevitable. This land will be developed. It's good land. Pilgrim Enterprises is proposing a well thought out plan that will benefit this town - our town. However, please, please, listen carefully. . . If this proposal is **not** approved by this Planning and Zoning Commission, this land will not just sit there. My clients will walk away and not exercise the purchase option they have on the property. Someone else will come in to buy it. **Something** is going to happen to it. If *we* don't develop it, someone else will, and . . . and . . . **you never know *who*, or *what*, that will be!"**

Chapter 2
THE HOT ATTORNEY

Attorney Cimione stepped back from the podium, nodded his head to Bradley and to the four seated Commissioners, and walked slowly back to his seat. An uneasy quiet settled over the crowd, creeping in like a heavy mist engulfing a Georgia swamp. People were digesting the attorney's closing remarks, the not-so-veiled sinister tone of his words. Cimione had used just enough inflection and innuendo to create a sense of apprehension in their minds. *What else could go on the land?* He inwardly smiled as he realized his thinly veiled comments were having their intended effect. He wanted people's imaginations *to conjure up whatever worst-case scenarios they could*, and to this end, he felt successful. "A good thought to close on, let them simmer on the devil they don't know," he murmured smugly to himself. "Bastards!'"

Cimione reached his seat, turned and collapsed into it, relieved to be away from the focal point of anger. He reached under his seat and grabbed a bottle of water, and drank profusely. Water dribbled down his chin. He stopped drinking, wiped his chin with his sleeve, and drew a long deep breath. He took out his crumbled handkerchief, squeezed some perspiration out of it, and again wiped the sweat off of his brow. His mind was racing. *What went wrong? Where did he lose control?* He had carefully planned for this hearing. He had done his homework; he had lined up all the right experts. His years of experience as a local attorney had taught him how to play the crowd, how to make arguments in front of the Planning and Zoning Commission, but tonight it wasn't clicking. He knew what had to be put into the record in the event of a court appeal, what words to use and what problems to address. He knew when to raise his voice and when to use soothing words. Tonight however, his efforts were futile, useless. Frustration engulfed him. *What went wrong?*

Slowly, like a summer mist rising, he realized that he had clearly underestimated the speed and intensity with which the opposition had developed. Just a few short weeks ago, he had heard that a few housewives in the adjacent neighborhood had gotten together over coffee and decided to organize and oppose the project. No big deal, just a few housewives with time on their hands, or so he had thought. Tonight, he realized, he had seriously underestimated them. The crowd's boisterous reaction tonight had proved just how seriously wrong he had been.

He focused his growing anger on Marcia Richards, one of the key organizers. He knew a little about her, having kept up on gossip in his years in Covingford. A mother of three, she only became involved in local government when it was time to vote for the school budget at the annual town meeting. However, in the short time since the shopping center hearing dates were publically announced, she had somehow organized her neighborhood, raised money from all the nearby houses that would be impacted, created a web site, started a blog, and, of all things, even hired their own attorney.

Belatedly, Cimione now realized that she had moved quickly, more quickly and resourcefully than he had given her credit for. Based on the new faces he saw tonight, he knew it was people she must have contacted since there were many residents who rarely became involved in local government. She had somehow prodded them into getting organized - probably met around her kitchen table to develop strategy- housewives, *desperate housewives!* He briefly laughed inwardly at his own reference to the TV show. He lowered his head and slowly shook it. He had underestimated the focus and intensity of their opposition, their commitment. They had a hard core commitment. Tax revenue for the town was not their issue. They had a cause, and their cause was saving their neighborhood-the enemy was at the gate.

Cimione was correct in that Marcia Richards had indeed organized a small group to meet at her house. The proposed development was just down the street from her home. She was concerned, very concerned. Many of the neighborhood children walked in that area to school. There was little traffic to worry about. It was very peaceful, an undisturbed open space area. She had called several neighbors, and held their first meeting in her kitchen. The response was overwhelming. Out of ten women all talking at once, a plan was hatched. A telephone and e-mail tree was established, with individuals assigned to reach out to other neighbors.

Marcia, although very pleased with the response and the enthusiasm of the group, had pointed out that they needed legal help for the upcoming public hearings. "My friend just went through a sticky divorce and her attorney was super," one of the women had offered "No nonsense type of a lawyer. She's done some planning and zoning work too. I remember her name in the paper several months ago when she fought against that big home improvement store that wanted to go into Northbury. Pat Burns, that's her name, a real scrapper. I'm sure she would love to represent us." Everyone around the table nodded their heads in agreement. "I'll work on a Facebook page and start tweeting to raise money," Marcia offered.

And thus the newly formed group made their bold move and decided to hire their own attorney to fight for their cause. Their choice was Patricia Burns, a divorce attorney with an office in nearby Middletown. Marcia made the call the next morning.

Cimione's thoughts over Marcia Richard's organizing maneuvers were suddenly interrupted by the banging of the gavel. He looked up and watched as Chairman Bradley spoke forcibly into the microphone. "Thank you Attorney Cimione. Before I call on Attorney Burns for her closing statement, I want to again remind you that this is our third consecutive night of hearings, and we've already been here over three hours. It is almost 11:00 o'clock." He grimaced, and looked out over the crowd. The other commissioners silently followed his gaze as he continued. "Everyone has had the opportunity both tonight and on the last two nights to make their feelings known. I am going to now call on Attorney Burns to **briefly** summarize her closing remarks. I realize it's late, and this room is hot!"

"Damn right it's hot," a voice blurted out, "and full of bullshit." Laughter erupted, followed by more murmurs and hissing, although at lower levels due to the long night. Bradley thankfully noted the weaker response.

Kurt Thomas sat off on one side, a place that allowed him to see not only the presentations, but to follow the reactions of the crowd. As Town Manager, he had listened intently to the arguments from both sides. He realized the public sentiment clearly had swung against the developers. He thought Attorney Cimione had presented the developer's proposal the first night in a good light, displaying extensive maps and sketches. The attorney had carefully structured his presentations. He and members of his expert team had made full presentations with brightly colored maps and detailed reports. Kurt was convinced at the end of the first night that they had made a positive presentation on a proposal that looked good for Covingford. The questions from the public had been answered directly and with little fanfare. The crowd's mood had been neutral. The attorney had emphasized the improvements to the vacant land, the expansion to the town's tax base, the additional employment. All were factors, he had stressed, that the town needed badly. The aging high school desperately needed major renovations, which would require issuing new municipal bonds and subsequently impacting taxes. Even Kurt had recently reminded the Town Council of the potential costs to renovate the high school, and at the same time, the new tax revenue stream the developer's proposal would create for the town. "Big property tax dollars, plus the employment opportunities," he had advised. Although one councilor asked for a fiscal analysis, several councilors had immediately enthusiastically endorsed the proposal. A few decided to take a wait and see attitude. Councilor Keith Mitchell, the Town Council's finance guru, had early on emphasized that new sources of revenue had to be found, especially with the high school renovations which would be costly, even with substantial State aid. "Barring any new economic development, local property taxes will have to be raised substantially," he had warned.

By the second night of the public hearing however, Kurt had sensed a swelling of opposition. Members of the public had raised numerous questions and objections. And despite a strong endorsement of the proposal from the local Chamber of Commerce and the Town's Economic Development Commission, the mood of the crowd, composed mostly of adjacent and nearby property owners, had shifted against the proposal. Jeers became common. Kurt felt sorry for Chairman Jim Bradley in his role as the meeting moderator. Kurt squirmed as he watched Bradley struggle with the crowd as it became more unruly with each speaker. Jim was a good meeting moderator, well experienced, and for him to have a problem indicated how difficult the crowd had become. And tonight, the third straight night of hearings, the crowd had become outright belligerent, cantankerous; the virtue of patience was conspicuous by its absence. Yes, Kurt realized, it was not a good night to be the developer, not by a long shot.

In the far back of the room Peter Gargano, a local contractor and key promoter of the project sat quietly, his rising blood pressure lighting up his round jocular face like a giant overripe tomato. His massive chest rose and fell quickly as he fought to control his temper. The gold chain around his neck seemed to glow brighter in contrast to his reddened face and colossal neck. "Open public meetings in New England are so damn unpredictable," he hoarsely whispered to his business partner and first cousin Salvatore. "One of these days we might even get to enjoy one - if we ever have the opportunity to attend just as citizens."

"Yeah, no shit Pete, but it ain't gonna be tonight," whispered Sal. "No fuckin way. Not tonight. Not with this crowd." Sal stroked his goatee in agitation. Shorter than his cousin, Sal carried the same muscular frame, hardened over the years by building construction. Despite his discomfort in his hot black shirt, he focused on the PZC Commission members who sat immobile in the front of the room. "Look at those commissioners, they're frozen, afraid of this goddam crowd-it's a mob for cripes sake."

"Fuck'em," Peter replied. "We can still get this through." Glancing around the room, he lowered his voice even more, "and when we get it through, it'll be a home run for us."

"Yeah, a home run," Sal responded sarcastically, "but right now it's the bottom of the ninth and there are two outs, and that Burns broad is about ready to give her closing statement."

" . . . Attorney Burns to briefly summarize her closing arguments," the loudspeakers in the rear of the room blared out Bradley's voice, snapping Peter and Sal out of their private conversation. Their eyes, along with everyone else's, turned toward the front of the room.

"Look at her strut up to the podium," Peter murmured to his cousin in a disgusted tone. "If she wears her damn skirt any shorter it'll be up over her ears."

"But man, she is really hot!"

Peter and Sal glared at Attorney Burns. They both had been surprised at the strength and force of her arguments on the previous night. Now they both watched intently, not saying a word. Peter's thoughts raced back over the last several months as he watched her move to the podium. *What had he missed?* Both he and his cousin had quietly made contact with several council members and members of the political town committees about the benefits of this project. These contacts, along with some financial contributions to some local politicians, had helped move the project quickly to this final stage. Most of the contacts had immediately seen the benefit of the shopping center to Covingford. "Now," simmered Peter to himself, "all of our background work, our meetings, our phone calls, our contributions, are threatened by a fast talking bitchy female attorney about to give her closing remarks."

Peter and Sal had heard the same arguments in many other towns - more traffic, congestion, "outsiders", veiled innuendos of the different types of people the project would attract, its impact on the school system, police services, fire demand - the list went on and on. Although each town was different, Peter realized that they were the same in so many ways. The names and faces changed, but the arguments stayed the same. And now, here in their hometown of Covingford, people they knew and saw daily were making the same arguments against the project they were supporting.

These same people, their neighbors, had suddenly taken on an attitude that astounded Peter. He understood that the residents realized that this was their last opportunity to make their feelings known, that this was the last night of the hearings. But still, the proposal was good for the town, what the hell was the matter with them? "Jerks! Stupid jerks!" he growled. He heard that the neighbors had been busy in the last week – posters, lawn signs, mailings, Facebook, even Tweeter, *whatever the hell that is*. Submitting petitions against the project to the Planning and Zoning Commission? And their name, their fuckin name - "Save What's Already There", or SWAT as they affectionately referred to themselves. *Assholes.*

Attorney Burns, ten years out of law school, had learned the importance of the emotional arguments at these heated meetings, especially when the emotion was generated on her side. She knew this and was ready for it as she reached the podium. Her flaming red hair seemed to brighten as every eye in the room focused on her petite five foot four inch frame. Her fiery eyes glowed. She carried herself with an air of confidence, inwardly knowing she was going to blow the roof off the cafeteria in the next few minutes. She reached for the microphone, and slowly adjusted it for her height. She was in no rush, she was in control. She had made her presentation on the second night of the hearing, citing the necessary statutes and the legal arguments on why the project should be denied. Tonight was the time to bury the project, time for the *coup de grace*. She smiled inwardly.

"Mr. Chairman, I realize the hour is late, so I will only make a brief closing statement." She paused and deliberately gazed around the room. The crowd was absolutely silent, anticipation hung in the air. Every eye in the room was on her as if she had cast a spell.

She had everyone's undivided attention- a lawyer's dream. The crushing heat and humidity in the cafeteria seemed to cease to exist. The intensity of her presence had encompassed them all. Their eyes focused only on the lady at the podium; the world outside had stopped. The wall clock ticked loudly in the still room as the minute hand crept past 11:00.

"Commissioners, town officials, ladies and gentlemen - tonight, Covingford is at a crossroads," she started in a low but firm voice, her eyes slowly scanning the packed cafeteria. "There is only one question remaining, just one single question." She stopped, timing her pause to perfection. "Will Covingford retain its local character, its home town flavor - all the things everyone in this room loves about this town, or. . . or will this project get approved for a few tax dollars?" Her voice raised a notch. "Covingford is a nice town, a quaint town, one that has been in existence for over 200 years, and yet, here we are, tonight, faced with a proposal that will change our way of life forever. It will increase traffic, pollute the environment, destroy trees and flowers, hurt our little family-run grocery store, crime surely will go up. . . Yes, our small town charm is at stake, threatened by a group that thinks they can waive tax revenues and jobs in our faces and we will welcome them with open arms. I think not."

"What's this 'our town' crap?" whispered Sal. "She doesn't even live here." He shook his head, disgusted. Peter just stared at the podium, a volcano building in his chest.

Attorney Burns again paused, gazing around the room. She knew she now had their undivided attention. The ticking of the clock blended with the swish of the circulation fans in the ceiling as they struggled to push the super saturated air back down on the crowd. Every eye was on the petite figure at the podium, the little lady whose brilliant red hair seemed to be on fire under the lights –every ear strained to hear her. She had control of the crowd, complete control.

Kurt had attended numerous meetings in his years as Town Manager and understood the dynamics of crowds. He realized that her timing and her delivery were extraordinary. He also noticed Peter and Sal, deep scowls on their faces, staring menacingly at her. Even Janet had stopped writing her newspaper notes and was looking up – mesmerized by the presence and the delivery of the fiery tiny woman at the front of the room.

"Citizens of Covingford," Burns bellowed, breaking the spell, "we have a long and proud history of self-government and stable development. We cannot allow our town to be ravaged - to lose our pristine open space, to abandon our small New England charm in one fell swoop." She hesitated. Her audience remained fixed on her every word, her slightest body movement - total fixation.

"Bullshit!" whispered Sal. "Fuckin' bullshit!" His dark black eyes bulged as his heavy eyebrows twitched like they had been touched with an electric current. "Pristine open space, my ass, it's a goddam open space dump!" Peter stared blankly ahead, shaking his head, muttering "pristine" over and over again, not believing what he just heard.

Shifting her feet, the diminutive fireball raised her voice another notch. "This proposal will bring in lots of outsiders, strangers, who knows what? Our open forest area will be lost forever. Do we really need another shopping center? This is big, way too big for Covingford. It threatens all of the qualities we hold to be so dear. For what? A few tax dollars? Some employment with lower paying jobs? The lining of the developers' pockets? No! I think not!" Her voice reached a tempo that carried a sense of urgency.

She turned slightly toward the PZC Commissioners on the stage with her, careful to keep the audience just to her right side where she could monitor their reactions. She focused intently on each commissioner. The commissioners returned her stare, mesmerized, waiting for her next bombshell. Nobody blinked. Burns knew they were the only ones who could vote on the project. Not the Zoning Board of Appeals nor the Town Council. Any appeal of their decision, affirmative or negative, would go directly to the courts. She clearly knew that the PZC was the local land use authority. They had authority over local land development. Their vote was critical.

"Commissioners, do not give away what we hold so dear. . . Save our town," she hesitated for effect. "End this proposal right here - right now - once and for all. Save what's already here! Save Covingford. . . Reject this monstrosity, this abomination. **Vote no**!" she thundered.

After a few seconds that seemed to go on forever, the crowd jumped to its feet, the roar was deafening. People laughed, cried, and nodded their heads. War hoops bellowed out. The tension of three nights had been broken and an emotional outburst spilled over onto everyone - or almost everyone - in the room. The stamping of feet and clapping of hands, somehow in unison, filled the school cafeteria and continued for a full three minutes.

The little old lady in the third row put down her knitting and began to cheer and clap. Tears rolled down her wrinkled face, dripping over the broad smile on her dry cracked lips. She shook her head slowly as she gazed fondly at Attorney Burns. *Such a nice lady, such a sweet nice lady, so glad we hired her. I will have to invite her over for tea and cookies. Hmmm, on second thought, let's make that scotch and cookies.*

Chapter 3
THE END OF THE HEARINGS

"Bitch," cursed Peter in a voice just loud enough for his cousin to hear. "Damn female lawyer bitch. . ." Peter's face was contorted with angry wrinkles, purple red veins bulged from his thick neck, his breath came in short bursts.

"What a bunch of crap," Sal spat out, hardly hearing his cousin. "She's worked this crowd into a fuckin' frenzy. Look at the goddam Commissioners- even they seem to have some doubts. This could be trouble, real trouble. This fuckin' project could even get denied!"

"No shit," Peter responded sarcastically.

"That'll be trouble, real trouble," Sal said again shaking his head, his face flush with a mixture of anger and frustration. "That bitch is jeopardizing everything."

Peter nodded in agreement, his eyes blazing with fury as he scanned the room. Everywhere he looked there seemed to be enemies-no friendly faces. "Look at these idiots, they're going bullshit." Both cousins glared at the turmoil in front of them. It bordered on a carnival atmosphere. Three boiling hours of pent up emotions had broken loose. People were talking, laughing, clapping, slapping one another on the back. The Commissioners remained fixed in their chairs, astounded by the reaction of the crowd. They tried to talk to one another, but the decibel level was too high. They gave up, sat back, and took in the scene before them. One Commissioner whispered to himself, "Wow, what a real humdinger of an old fashion New England public meeting! Haven't seen this much action in a long long time. Television certainly cannot hold a candle to this pandemonium. Look at this mob!"

"Let's get the hell outta here," Peter said as he stood up and started for the exit. He ignored the annoyed looks from the several residents he abruptly pushed aside.

Although not as vocal as his cousin, Sal's thoughts were the same – total disgust and anger. And at that moment, both business partners had one person at the top of their hate list -Attorney Burns—head and shoulders above all the others. And they had a long list, a very long list, one that had accumulated over years of aggravation and fighting to ensure they got their own way.

Sal started after his cousin, almost running to catch up. "I'll make some more phone calls," Sal said in short breaths, as he caught his cousin. Their rush to the exit was slowed however by the number of other people also leaving the cafeteria. The moderator was still in the front of the room talking, but few seemed to be listening. Sal caught his breath and said, "I'll call some of the damn Town Councilors first thing in the morning, wake them up if I have to. They may have to lean on the Commissioners that they've appointed. Where the hell is the "Bomb" when we need him?"

"Dom's still over on the side where the snacks are," Peter retorted without turning his head. "Right in the section where the lighting ain't too good, probably so he can't see how much, or what, he's eating."

"Good place for him-lots of food and little light, nuttin' gonna help his fat flabby looks," replied Sal sarcastically.

"He didn't look none too happy either," Peter replied

"No surprise. His big fat ass is on the line on this one, big time," Sal said.

"Wait a minute," Peter said brusquely. "Something's wrong. None of the damn PZC or Council members spoke up tonight." He stopped so abruptly that Sal banged into him. Sal's glasses, dropped off his face, dangling from one ear. He quickly adjusted them. Peter disregarded the collision. "The damn town officials didn't say squat tonight on the project. Zero. Nothing. Nada. Niente. It's a fuckin' public hearing. The Commissioners just sat on the stage looking like they were comatose, didn't say shit. Matter of fact, same with the Town Manager."

Sal stopped abruptly and turned to Peter. "Pete, remember, it's the PZC that votes on the project, not the Council or the Manager. The Commissioners can't state their views during the public hearings, you know that. They don't want to be accused of being prejudiced. After the hearings close, they can talk and discuss it till the cows come home at their next public meetings, express their viewpoints publically, and then vote on it. Don't worry too much yet. Remember our Town Council members have been mostly in favor of the project, especially the ones we had a chat with," Sal continued with a wry grin as he stared at Peter, again adjusting his glasses. "With the strong public objection tonight, they are probably afraid to take a stance favoring the project. Goddam politicians. But, don't forget, I've been working with a few key Council members who are totally behind this project, and I mean totally. Councilor Mitchell is 100% on board, and he is a strong member of the Council. As for the Town Manager, he's just playing it safe, although early on he was leaning in favor of it."

"He's a pussy. Son-of-a- bitch! Even without a vote, that bastard is influential. We need to keep an eye on him too," Peter said angrily as they both turned again to the outer doors.

"The PZC is the key though, they are the ones who vote. Not all these jerks around us," Sal whispered derisively.

"Yeah, they may do the actual voting," Peter responded, " but don't underestimate the influence of the Council since they appoint them."

"No shit, but they're politicians, and they can be swayed by the damn public, especially when the public is loud and, based on tonight's debacle, that could be a problem, a real fuckin' problem! " Sal said disgustedly.

Both cousins finished weaving through the crowd and slipped through the exit into the dimly lit parking lot. Peter took a deep breath of the February air. He pulled up the collar of his overcoat against the nipping frigid temperature. "Damn, it's cold out here, but it feels good after that oven, what a hothouse. Damn school needs air conditioning." Billows of hot air escaped from his lungs, forming large clouds of condensation in the light falling snow.

"That's for sure-that room was like a furnace," Sal said, as he strode side by side with his cousin. "Look, I'll call Mitchell and a few other members of the Council again to make sure that they lean on the Commissioners. They need to remind the Commissioners of the importance of this project to the town, especially after tonight!"

"And the importance to our construction company," Peter snickered, "tons of work for us for the next two years."

"And let's not forget our investors," Sal added with wry grin. "Shit, and let's not forget the Town Manager. We don't want him wavering. He needs to be reminded that this is critical for the town. I don't want him spouting off - too many people listen to him."

"We're all gonna have to lean a little harder on the PZC Commissioners. As for the Town Manager, he can be a pain in the ass, a little too independent." Peter continued, and then in a lower sinister tone, "But he works directly for the Council, and he ain't protected by some goddam labor union. As they say, he's an 'at will' employee."

"Yeah, he needs to be reminded of that." Sal snickered. "And Mitchell is the one to do it. Nothing like a little pressure from one of your bosses to make a point."

"Yes! And there are ways to make his life more difficult if need be," Peter said menacingly as he and Sal reached their car, "and Mitchell can be a master at that." They reached their new black Cadillac, covered in a light snow. Peter hit the remote and the light inside the car flashed on, illuminating the dark area around the car. Sal reached into the back seat and grabbed the brush to clear the windows. Numerous cars around them had started and were warming up, their exhausts pouring out into the cool night air, scrubbed clean by the falling snow.

Inside the building, Jim Bradley, filled with relief, saw that the crowd had quieted down and people were leaving. He knew he had to formally close the hearing even though most people assumed it was already over. He took the microphone and said in a firm steady voice, "This Commission will now review the record, weigh all of the evidence, and make its decision within 65 days at a meeting that will be open to the public. However, with the close of this hearing tonight, no further public input will be accepted. This hearing is now closed to further comment. We stand adjourned," he exclaimed with a final bang of the gavel. This time there were no cheers, no boos.

The four other PZC members on the stage all experienced a wave of relief. Despite having made no comments during the hearing, they knew the spotlight was now on them. "Nice job Jim," one of them commented to Bradley. "This was a tough crowd, but you controlled the tempo." Jim smiled fleetingly and nodded his head in acknowledgement. His insides were like butterflies.

Its energy spent, the crowd continued to exit the room, making its way into the parking area. Clear cold air blasted their faces, bringing a wave of relief and a refreshing contrast. Small pockets of people lingered in the cafeteria, and continued to talk as they relived the drama of the evening. Most however, just scurried to their cars. The hour was late and there was work tomorrow.

Lingering behind in a corner of the room, Marcia Richards' small group continued to talk, all at once. No one seemed to care that nobody was listening. "We won! We won!" "We beat 'em!" "Boy did we beat them, we kicked their ass." The fact that the Commission had not yet voted on the proposal hardly seemed to matter. Their hastily organized anti-development campaign had succeeded beyond their wildest expectations, and they were drunk with its success. "The Commission won't dare approve the project after tonight! We fought city hall and won," Marcia exclaimed with tears in her eyes. "Marcia for Mayor!" one of the women gushed out. "Hear, hear" was the immediate response. Marcia smiled sheepishly and turned to their attorney. "Patty, you were wonderful, just wonderful! Our hero. What great arguments." The neighbors around her nodded in complete agreement and cheered some more. Patty just smiled, soaking up the adulations with a deep sense of accomplishment. She shared their feeling of complete victory! *Yes*, she thought, *tonight was our night.*

The happiest person at that moment, however, was not the Commissioners, nor Marcia's group, nor the attorneys, not even the little old lady in the third row. No, the happiest person at the final bang of the gavel was Nick Brown, the night custodian. His shift was almost over, and with the hearing closed, he could now get out before it got too late. He watched the crowd slowly dissipate, and then flicked a few overhead lights to give a not-so-subtle hint that it was time to close up the building. Marcia's group continued to talk, too excited to notice the flicking. Nick's only interest at that moment however, was not the heat of the battle, the future of Covingford, nor the arguments or counter arguments - no - right now Nick was totally focused on his easy chair at home, the late night World War II movie on Channel 8, and the cold beer waiting for him in his refrigerator - that ice cold frosty beer. "Yeah," he said aloud to himself with a grin on his face, "as soon as I move these people and set the alarm, I'm outta here. Time to go home. *It's Miller time.*"

Chapter 4
DOMINIC'S VISITOR

Dominic "the Bomb" Columbo waddled through the crowd and exited the school. Even to the Bomb, the blast of the frigid winter air felt refreshing. He slowly made his way to the far end of the school parking lot, his baggy drooping pant cuffs dragging through the snow covered ground. To the casual observer, his brown camel hair coat presented an image of the animal for which the material was named. His ragged loafers squished down on the snow, groaning under the three hundred pounds they supported.

In his mid-forties with a five-foot-five stature, Dominic was mostly bald, with just a ring of black hair on the top. If he had worn a long waist cord, he could have obtained a role in the movies as a Middle Ages monk. Strong red Italian wine with dinner was his drink of choice, and an occasional beer in the summer. He avoided hard liquor, "Not healthy" he always joked. The top button on his shirt was never used, a perfect match to his half tied food-spotted tie that dropped loosely around his 19" neck. His love of food displayed in his 55-inch waist, which, at his height, was almost double his twenty-eight inch inseam, a ratio that insured he could not buy his clothes "off the rack." He was a regular customer at Mario's, the local tailor who had the onerous task of altering everything to fit the man. To his trusted customers, Mario had jokingly coined the phrase "Dom the Blimp," a tag that quietly spread in the community, although never to Dominic's face. It did offer an amusing comic relief to the public who had their own perception of "Dom The Bomb." Dominic, oblivious to the "Blimp" mantra, relished in the "Bomb" nickname, which, in his own little world, he felt described himself.

Late for the hearing, Dominic had to park his long black old Lincoln on the far end of the parking lot. The moonless night was as dark as deep outer space, and the falling snow obscured what little light came from the aging meager lighting in the school parking lot. Slowly lumbering in the darkness to the remote areas where he had been forced to park, he slipped on the light coating of snow. "Damn. I'm chairman of the town committee. They should've at least reserved a parking space for me up front, sons-of-bitches!" He finally reached his car, and squeezed the remote button. Nothing happened. "Damn, I gotta get the damn battery replaced in this remote." He inserted the key into the frozen lock. The door reluctantly gave up its protective status with a slow click. He tugged on the handle, and the door opened with a groan from its own tired weight. The dim interior car ceiling light barely lit his snow covered camel jacket.

Dominic lowered his massive body onto the seat with a thud, the coldness of the torn leather penetrated into his pants. His heavy breathing formed clouds of mist in front of him. Fumbling to find the key for the ignition, he pondered the many phone calls and meetings he had held in the last few weeks with key political figures. Now, all his work seemed to be in jeopardy. Finally inserting the key, the overhead light in his car went out as the engine reluctantly groaned to start. He sat back and took a deep wheezing breath, and mumbled out loud, "Now I got to get out again and brush off this damn snow. And that goddam bitch attorney-she needs a good screwing to straighten her out."

"Bad show tonight Dominic. Maybe you need a screwing!"

"What. . . what . . ." Startled, Dominic's heart skipped a beat. He started to turn his head, but before he could turn his massive neck, a gloved hand harshly covered his gaping mouth.

"Shut up and just listen" the menacing male voice growled, sending shivers down Dominic's body. He began to shake uncontrollably under the cold grip of the unrelenting glove, suddenly regretting where he parked. There was no one else around.

The hand loosened its grip on his face and dropped to his bulging neck. "You know what happens if this project fails?"

"It'll pass. . . It'll pass." Dominic exclaimed hastily as he worked his jaw that was stiff from the grip of the glove. He instantly recognized the voice, Louie "The Enforcer." He knew who the ominous person represented, and he knew the Enforcer's reputation! Dominic wiped the saliva from the corners of his mouth, tasting the leather from the intruder's glove. He swallowed hard several times. "I'm, . . I'm gonna take care of things. No shit. I'll make more calls to the Commissioners and. . . and . . . I'll remind them of a few things they want to forget – things they REALLY want to forget."

"Maybe it's you that people will want to forget," the voice said with a sneer.

Dominic shook again, shivers racking his massive frame. "I know things, nasty things. I . . . I can help sway their thinking."

"They better see your way of thinking."

"They . . . they will." Dominic said in a pleading tone. His chest suddenly felt tight, his breathing was short and quick. The three hundred pounds of fat shook the tired springs of the Lincoln's frame. The windshield completely fogged up.

"Sounds like a lot of hot air to me. I think you're blowing smoke."

"No, no I'm not. I'll, I'll make more calls tonight, soon as I get home. " Dominic continued.

"What about the Town Manager? Bet you'se got nothin on him. He not a local, comes from out-of-town, an outsider."

"No problem. I already called a few of the Town Council members about him. They'll keep him in line, especially one councilor. They hired him and they can fire him."

"Do what you have to do. . ."

"I . . . I will. No problem. It will get approved. You'll see." Dominic pleaded in a desperate tone, trying to gain some composure. The engine of the big Lincoln purred quietly, despite its 150,000 miles of hard labor. Its exhaust formed a large cloud of moisture in the cold dry New England air.

"This project had better get approved by the town - for your sake, and. . . and that of the pretty little wife of yours." The gloved hand tightened slightly on Dominic's neck.

Dominic nodded his head rapidly, his throat too dry to respond.

Without another word, the "Enforcer" opened the rear door and slipped out of the back seat. He carefully closed the door, turned and was immediately swallowed up by the foreboding dark night. Dominic did not turn, but sat as though frozen, staring blankly ahead. He knew what the conversation meant. His rotund stomach ached and he fought to keep down the bile that was forming in his throat. The heavy Lincoln continued to shake.

Thursday February 28
RESIDENTS BLAST PROPOSAL
"COVINGFORD CHARM" IN JEOPARDY
By Janet Johnson
Inquirer Staff Reporter

COVINGFORD - An angry overflow crowd of more than 250 people jammed into the cafeteria of Covingford High School to hear the final presentation by Pilgrim Associates, a development group proposing a major shopping center in the Northeast corner of town. Last night was the third night of the public hearings being conducted by the Planning and Zoning Commission. After a final presentation by local attorney Richard Cimione on behalf of the developers, Attorney Patricia Burns tore apart the proposal. Attorney Burns, representing a neighborhood group opposing the project, made an inflamed attack on the proposal. "Covingford will lose its small town New England charm," she claimed. She pleaded with the Commissioners to "Save our Town. End this proposal right here, right now." At the end of her speech, the crowd roared its approval of her diatribe.

The shopping center to be built on 25 acres of undeveloped land off of Goose Lane, involves a major anchor store and several smaller retail stores. "This proposal will impact traffic in our neighborhood, increase crime, accidents, hurt local businesses, and result in a loss of open space," according to Marcia Richards, organizer of the neighborhood group "Save What's Already There (SWAT). Her organization is fighting the project, and they hired Attorney Burns.

Although several town officials were present, none of them spoke either for or against the proposal. Commissioner Chairman Jim Bradley closed the hearings at 11:15PM. The Commission has 65 days to reach a decision on the proposal.

Chapter 5
TOWN MANAGER AND NEWSPAPER REPORTER

Thursday February 28

The sign on the glass door leading into the reception area office simply stated "Town Manager." Although the secretary would normally first greet a visitor, an angry taxpayer could still quickly bypass her and confront the Town Manager in his office. Fortunately, the office, like many offices of mayors and other top officials, had its own rear exit, an important safety factor. On more than one occasion, it had proven to be a lifesaver for Kurt Thomas.

A small round table occupied a corner in Kurt's office, its main focus was to encourage visitors to sit in a more informal setting. Next to it, a small table held the ever-present coffee pot. The fragrance of the dark French Roast coffee permeated the office. Kurt frequently invited his visitors to sit at the round table with him and enjoy a cup of the fresh brew, a simple gesture that often diffused a volatile situation.

Kurt's desk was buried under an avalanche of numerous files, each one containing notes and memos on the many projects in which the town was involved. The less pressing projects were in files neatly piled on the credenza adjacent to the desk. Both flat areas performed their task as extensive horizontal files

On some days it seemed to Kurt that no real work got done, just meetings back to back, separated by the constant barrage of telephone calls. Numerous plaques and newspaper articles involving several different town issues covered the walls. Photos of the original senior center when it was converted from an elementary school in the 60's hung off to one side. Copies of Covingford's Annual Reports from recent years were stacked on the bookshelves. Notebooks containing several years of Town Council minutes and agendas filled the bookcases along the wall. They contained the history of the Town Council's meetings, the legacy of the town's governing body. Stark bleak binders in their black format, holding the history in cold written words of so many emotional wrenching hotly debated issues. In effect, they were a virtual compendium of all of the official actions of the Council – important critical life-changing decisions, or so it seemed at the time.

"Kurt, I have Janet Johnson on line two," Liz Kelsey, Kurt's secretary, said in a raspy voice, breaking into Kurt's train of thought. The sharp buzz of the telephone intercom had startled Kurt. His office, a large room filled with bookcases, a computer, old oak desk, and a round meeting table, was located on the second floor of the Town Hall. "She wants to ask you a question on last night's public hearing for her story. And . . . as usual," Liz paused to emphasize her irritation at the reporter's request for immediate access to the Manager, "she has to talk to you right now so she can make her deadline for tomorrow's edition." Liz made no attempt to hide her lack of patience with the reporter's attitude.

"Do I detect a note of annoyance in your voice?" Kurt asked teasingly as he brushed his hair back with his hand. Strands of gray were evident against the dark brown combed hair.

"Just a tad. All reporters seem to think they are the only ones with deadlines to meet," Liz responded in exasperation. "Although I will admit she is better than most of the other reporters we have had to deal with, but she STILL has an attitude."

"Thanks Liz, I'll pick up that call right now," Kurt replied. He tucked the phone on his right shoulder and held it in place with his tilted head. Liz, sensing her complaints were falling on deaf ears, muttered something under her breath that fortunately for her, Kurt could not quite hear. Having a good idea she had muttered, Kurt grinned and automatically reached for a pen so he could start taking notes. The habit had become one of necessity after years of dealing with dozens of people every day, each with a different issue or problem, and often with differing opinions. Kurt knew that a short pencil was better than a long memory.

"Morning Janet."

"Hi Kurt, how are you this morning?" Janet's greeting was crisp and cheerful. "Thanks for taking my call."

"No problem. I'm doing fine considering the lateness of last night's meeting." Kurt responded in a noncommittal tone, notebook in hand. His guard was already up, as was his style in dealing with reporters, especially with Janet since she had a very disarming manner. He clearly pictured her in his mind: well-proportioned figure, tight ponytail and wire rimmed glasses that reminded him of Lois Lane in the old Superman movies. Her eyes, coupled with her tiny nose that turned up slightly at the end and little dimples, gave her the appearance of a cute young school aged co-ed, although Kurt guessed she was in her early forties. Her glasses emphasized a soft set of bedroom brown eyes, so soft that Kurt was sure they had entrapped many a person being interviewed. He knew that behind the impish look was a mind like a high-speed computer, coupled with a steel-trap memory. On more than one occasion he had read her stories and was amazed at the level of detail and information she had accumulated.

"That certainly was an agitated crowd," Janet offered in a smoothing tone.

"That's an understatement." Kurt replied, realizing that Janet's probe for information had already started. He felt a twang of uneasiness. "Saw your article in this morning's paper. You must have enough information to write articles for the Inquirer for a week." Kurt knew that Janet had a good handle on the politics of the meetings and the personalities involved.

"I do have a lot of material Kurt. However, if I printed all of the comments and accusations, there would be a flurry of lawsuits against the paper and myself. I don't think my editor would be too happy."

"And we certainly don't want your editor to be unhappy, do we?" he teased.

"No we do not," she responded emphatically. "And speaking about last night, people were really worked up. That crowd was jumping. I think Pat Burns did quite a remarkable job on her closing statement before the PZC - the audience loved it, that's for sure."

"And I'm sure the developers hated her theatrics," Kurt responded in a guarded tone.

"Does that mean you're in favor of the proposal?" Janet coyly asked. She smiled to herself, realizing that she had, in the first minute, already put Kurt in a defensive posture.

"No Janet, I do *not* mean that," Kurt emphatically replied with a note of irritation. He immediately pictured the headlines Janet could create from even a simple reply by him on that loaded question. *Town Manager in favor of proposed project - Citizens Group Demands his Resignation.* "No, not at all," he continued. "I'm just stating the facts based on the information I have. I know the work and money the developers have put into the shopping center proposal. They have been working at it for months, and I'm sure there were numerous strategy meetings." Kurt put his pen down, realizing the direction the conversation was taking. He took a brief sip of his steaming coffee. Colombian French Roast coffee, nice and strong, just the way he liked it, especially after a late night meeting.

"Like meetings involving the Garganos, or even the party chairman Columbo?" Janet asked with a devilish tinge to her voice. She was enjoying the conversation, her reporter instincts coming out. *Always fun to have an interviewee on the defensive, even if it was Kurt.* "They were all there last night, so I thought I'd check with you to see if you want to be quoted on their presence at the hearing."

"Nice try." Kurt responded with a quick nervous laugh. *Boy, she's quick.* "You know I'd never comment on the presence or absence of political characters like that. You'll have to try your other sources."

"How about one small comment about your friend, Dom Columbo?" Janet persisted.

"The Bomb? Not *my* friend! Gimme me a break!" Kurt responded, irritated at himself for reacting so quickly.

Janet laughed at the spontaneous reaction from Kurt. She knew what buttons to push. "Just thought I'd try anyway" she said sheepishly. "He always seems to have something to say about you, although seldom on the record."

"I'm sure. I trust him as far as I could throw his 300 pounds."

"You're off the record, of course?"

"You know that."

"O.K. Kurt, you get a pass this time." Changing the tone in her voice, she continued. "Seriously though, I was impressed last night with the intensity of the crowd and the lineup of political figures in the room. Do you know if the Garganos actually have a financial stake in the project or are they just trying to exert a little political influence by their presence at the hearing? The word on the street is that no big project gets approved in this town unless they are in favor of it. And," she hesitated and then in a lowered voice, "and since they jointly own a construction company, may have more than just a passing interest in this, like a big, big, construction contract."

"Very interesting." *Leave it to a reporter to pick up on things.* "And on what street did you hear that?" Kurt asked, intentionally trying to avoid a direct response.

"Come on Kurt, don't play games. I'm not going to quote you."

Picking his words carefully, Kurt responded. "They're an important political force in Covingford, that's for sure. I wouldn't go so far as to say that they control every big project that comes along, but. . .

". . . But they do control." Janet made a little squiggly note on her pad.

"Let me say this. I wouldn't want them fighting a project I wanted to get through. They know the system. It's taken years for them to develop their network."

"Their network? Are you saying they have a lot of IOUs out there?"

"Definitely off the record. . . yes, that's what I'm saying."

"OK Kurt, let's both of us go off the record. Just background information. No attribution."

"Agreed."

"I hear they have money, mucho money," Janet said, implying she had inside information.

"Sure do. Not only that, they've employed numerous residents over the years in their construction company, and have helped many people through hard times. They give freely of their time, are very active in the community. The fact that their fathers were brothers and the two families all grew up in the same neighborhood in South Hartford gives them lots of local contacts. Plus, they have strong political ties to people at the state level. Powerful combinations." Kurt paused and took another sip of his coffee. *Still nice and hot. Nothing like the aroma of the robust coffee.* He loved strong coffee in the morning and although he had stopped smoking over ten years ago right after his divorce, he still sorely missed the taste of the morning cigarette with his coffee.

"Not ones that you would want to have to fight?" Janet inquired.

"No question about it." Kurt responded, wondering where this line of questioning was now going. *She certainly knows her business.* He stood up and walked around his desk. He sat on the corner of the desk and glanced out the window. The street, two stories below, was busy with the morning rush. People were bundled up against the February cold that had gripped all of Connecticut. Salt stained cars moved slowly, their tires squeezing out the snowy slush.

"Well, I'm going to do some more digging on their presence last night. I suspect it was more than just a political interest. Did you notice that they weren't sitting close to Dominic at the meeting?"

"Yes, I did. Curious, wasn't it?" *Damn, she doesn't miss a trick.*

"Yes, especially since they seem to work together a lot." She continued.

"Yup, they are all in the same political party, and, from what I hear, there were all friends in grammar school. And I don't know which tie is stronger," Kurt added.

"Interesting!"

Kurt could picture Janet scribbling quick notes on her pad. "Don't underestimate the ties that are there. There are a lot of stories about that unholy trio - Sal, Peter and Dom. I've heard some real stories, especially about Columbo. Real sleazy stuff. He supposedly keeps company with people that even the Feds would like to know more about."

"Just don't underestimate him, Janet," Kurt said in a lowered voice to emphasize caution. "Underneath his three hundred pounds and sloppy manner is a very slick deceitful character."

"Really mendacious, to use our favorite newspaper term," Janet interrupted.

"Mendacious, isn't that like deceitful?"

"Very good," exclaimed Janet in a gleeful tine.

"Dom, he's not the sharpest pencil in the pack. But, he has a mind as quick as a snake and movements like a weasel. And his memory is better than all of your little notepads put together, *especially* if there is any dirt attached." Kurt glanced out at the outer office at his secretary. Liz was busy opening the morning mail. No one else was in the office.

"So I've heard." Janet replied. "I've also heard that he's been known to use information to maneuver people, embarrass them, trick them, manipulate them - anything to get what he wants. No scruples whatsoever. No moral compass."

"A real sweetheart," Kurt said. "He loves to use information to embarrass people. Maybe that's how he got the nickname "The Bomb.'"

"Very interesting. The Bomb's history! I've heard from several sources that he is devious. I'm going to try and explore that a little more. Maybe some of the neighbors at the hearing last night will want to add some other background information if he's involved. That type of information is tough to keep quiet."

"The neighbors probably don't really know him, unless they're involved in politics. And most of them aren't. Many will recognize his name, but for the most part, he doesn't get involved socially unless it's involving politics. Most probably don't even know what his political role is. They are busy with their own work and families. Generally they don't get involved in town politics, which is fine with Dominic. He prefers to operate in the shadows. Doesn't like his name in the newspaper unless it is some nice item. . ."

"Like his saving that abandoned puppy?" Janet inserted.

"Yeah, stuff like that. I did see your article on him and the rescue dog. Didn't know where that angle came from."

"Suggestion from my editor," Janet said almost apologizing.

"Dom's strange. He cares more about animals than people. He went out of his way to save that dog, spent money at the vets on shots and its broken leg. It's a real focus for him. Too bad he doesn't do as much for his fellow human beings." Kurt paused for a moment, gathering his thoughts. "He's not a public official, but he does influence public policy, often more than the elected officials that. . ."

"How does he influence public policy? Let's go on the record Kurt."

Boy, she's a pain. "I'm not going to comment on the record, Janet. Let's just say that he does have enough contacts and political connections to affect public policy and public decisions. He works hard at it. It is a thankless job. And, he's not even a town official – not elected, not appointed- but he is a force to be reckoned with. Really ticks me off that a character like that influences town affairs. He. . ." Kurt abruptly stopped, angry with himself for his reaction.

Janet said nothing.

"I've said enough for now, anything else?"

"Sorry Kurt, didn't mean to set you off," Janet responded in a slow sincere tone. "It is just an incredibly interesting area."

"That guy just gets to me-such a sleaze ball."

"You're not the first person to say that Kurt," Janet said quietly. "You know, it could be fun to write an article about him, a little lime-light, so to speak. I'll certainly mention him as background material on the public hearings, and see if I can dig anything else up on him."

"Just be careful Janet," Kurt said in a cautionary tone.

"Thanks Kurt. I appreciate that." After a pause, she continued. "I am also getting vibes on the land that the developers want to build on, something funny about it."

"Funny like how?" Kurt asked, his interest suddenly on full alert.

"Funny like an open space with very little wildlife on it, almost a dead zone-strange."

Kurt said nothing.

"Kurt, still there?" Janet asked in cryptic tone.

"Oh, yes, still here, was just digesting what you said about the land. That's all."

Puzzled by Kurt's reaction, Janet continued. "Ok Kurt, I think I'll give Jim Bradley a call. As chairman of the PZC, I am sure he's on top of everything, and, he may also have some interesting tidbits for me from last night's meeting."

"Up to you Janet, not sure how much he will say since his Commission now has to debate and vote on the project."

"I'll give it a shot. Let's change topics, anything exciting on Monday's Town Council meeting? I hope everyone is not too tired from last night's zoning hearing, it did run late."

"Looking for a big story for tomorrow?" Kurt blew the steam off of his coffee, glancing up briefly to see Liz in the outer office looking at him, her eyes rolling, a disgusted look on her face. He smiled for he knew that she just had no patience for news report-ers' continual questions. And she didn't hide her feelings!

"I already have my story for tomorrow, which will be a follow up to today's brief article. Wait till you see it," Janet said enthusiastically. Kurt sensed that she was experiencing the thrill reporters get when they spice up their stories with personal comments readers could relate to.

"I got some great comments after the meeting from some of the citizens. Our readers are going to love these stories," Janet continued gleefully.

"Why do I get the feeling that the developers are going to hate it?"

"News is news. I only report it. Back to Monday's meeting, anything hot on the Town Council agenda?" Janet persisted.

"No Janet," Kurt answered. "Hate to disappoint you, but it shouldn't be too exciting. Trash contract is on the agenda, but we are not ready for a report on it. Might just table it."

"Hey, maybe I'll get lucky and some big controversy will erupt," Janet said with a laugh.

"I've seen short agendas turn into long meetings when a group of citizens showed up and started focusing on a problem," he offered. Glancing outside, Kurt noticed one of the blue police cruisers turning the corner as it made its way back to the Town Hall. It was partially dirty white from the winter road salt. He made a mental note to tell the Police Chief to get the cruiser washed. He wondered how the rest of the fleet looked. The winter salt on the roads always took their toll on the vehicles.

"Well, I'll plan on covering it anyway. Maybe something will come up about last night's public hearing since some of the Council members were there. I'd like to get a quote from some of them. Like I said, maybe I'll get lucky."

"Never know when one is going to get lucky," Kurt replied in a deadpan tone.

Janet did not reply immediately. After an embarrassing pause, she hesitantly asked, "Kurt . . . How did you mean that?"

"I . . . I just meant, that – that you never know when you will find a story. That's all," Kurt stammered. He felt flushed, embarrassed.

"Oh, ok." Janet responded hesitantly and in a disappointing tone that baffled Kurt. "Talk to you later." The line went dead.

Kurt sat back in his chair, still holding the phone. He reviewed his conversation with Janet, especially the last few minutes. He absentmindedly twirled the last remnants of the coffee in the warm cup, thinking to himself. *Why had she asked about the condition of the land? Typical reporter, she just wants information to flow in one direction. Never fully reveals her hand, always seemed to have an ace up her sleeve.* He admitted to himself that she certainly knew how to put a story together, and could needle someone with just a few key words. *A "but" here, a "however" in the right place, and wham, the person was on the ropes. The power of a good grasp of the English language certainly is a powerful tool – or a weapon.* His eyes drifted around the office as he thought about Janet, her style, her writings, her impish mannerism, her penchant for the story behind the story. Although they spoke frequently on town business, he knew little, very little, about her personal life other than the fact she was also divorced, having been married for seven years to an FBI agent who was always on the road. Her job now was to report on public issues, and that included him as a public official. Yes she was impish, and attractive, very attractive. Cute as a button. *Too bad, really too bad, she's a news reporter!*

Chapter 6
PHONE CALL, COUNCIL MEMBER AND TOWN MANAGER

Thursday, February 28

Kurt sat at his desk, swirling the coffee cup in hand. He pondered Janet's question on whether there was anything exciting on the upcoming Council meeting. Had he missed something? He picked up the official agenda for the meeting. It had just been filed with the Town Clerk, thereby insuring the meeting notice met the State's Sunshine Law of at least 24 hours written notice prior to the actual meeting. Scanning the page, he tried to figure out if there were any real topics that could give rise to blaring headlines in the next few days. His answer came almost immediately, not from the agenda, but from the ring of the private line into his office. Calls on that line meant it was either a member of the Town Council, the Town Attorney, or his tennis partner.

"Kurt, this is Mitchell," came the sharp curt voice of Council member Keith Mitchell.

"Hi Keith." *So much for pleasantries.* "What's up?" Kurt knew Mitchell only too well. He could picture him on the other end of the line, all business. A man in his early-forties, almost six-foot, lean and wiry, black straight hair frozen in place with hair spray, and at this moment, a very agitated tone to his voice.

"Hell of a zoning hearing last night," Mitchell immediately said. "That chick lawyer was off the wall. She should be disbarred for her comments on the pristine open space! Pristine my ass! Maybe she is blind and we don't know it. Maybe, just maybe, she could get a job on Broadway." Mitchell made no attempt to hide the disgust and anger in his voice.

Kurt could picture Mitchell's crimson face full of fierce anger. He realized that the Councilor had malice on his mind with this phone call. He knew that when Mitchell made up his mind about something, any argument against him would be futile. "It's her job to be zealous," Kurt responded in a non-committal tone. Ignoring the remark, Mitchell continued. "This is a big project, really big for Covingford, and we don't want a smart-ass lawyer or even worse, a female smart-ass lawyer, screwing it up. Pristine open space, horseshit! Damn, she certainly gets press coverage though!"

"Saw the articles" Kurt injected. "And I am sure there'll be another one. Janet just told me she had interviewed several residents after the hearing broke up. She wanted to get their take 'on the flavor' of the meeting."

"Flavor! Flavor! How about pure unadulterated bull shit! Anything to sell papers. A female conspiracy. A goddamn female attorney screwing everything up, and then a female reporter reporting on it. The great screw-up duo. Pains in the ass, both of them."

"Janet's just doing her job as a reporter," Kurt responded almost defensively. *What the hell am I defending her for?*

"Maybe, but she better not stir things up any more than they already are. There's a lot at stake here for Covingford. It could be a big boost to our tax rolls, really big. Help this Council keep the tax rate down."

Kurt smiled to himself at the not too veiled comment on tax increases, especially since this coming November were local elections. "That's what the PZC has to weigh and decide," Kurt responded, trying to delicately remind the Councilor that the Town Council did not control everything.

Ignoring the comment, Mitchell continued. "Have you completed that fiscal analysis on the proposal to show how much tax money it will generate for Covingford?"

"We're evaluating the developer's data, both tax wise and cost wise. However, the big unknown is the real impact on the adjacent neighborhood, especially the traffic. They will be the ones most impacted"

"There's *always* traffic," Mitchell replied sarcastically. "Who knows, if this gets turned down, the next proposal could be even worse, without the tax benefit."

Kurt did not reply. *Interesting, same remark Attorney Cimione made in his closing remarks at the hearing.*

"Let me know as soon as you finish your analysis, and before you release it to the press. UNDERSTAND?" Keith said in a threatening tone.

"Yes." Kurt replied, always amazed at the rudeness of Mitchell's calls. "I'll have it ready in about two weeks or so and I'll send it just to the Town Council."

"That's right. I want it first and before it is on the Council agenda and becomes public!" Keith curtly retorted. *Just in case I have to make some suggestions for changes,* Keith thought sinisterly.

"Keith, you know my policy," Kurt replied emphatically. "If I send it to one Council member, it goes to all the Council members, at the same time. I work for all of you."

"Yea, yea. That's fine. I just don't like surprises, especially on such a big project. So let's not have any press releases from your office. It is a policy issue, so just send it to the Council before it is formally put on the agenda. It goes to us before anyone else. Don't overstep your bounds. Remember, as you say, you work for us." The warning tone in Mitchell's voice was unmistakable.

"Understood," Kurt replied in an exasperated tone.

"All right. Now, for Monday night's meeting, I intend to introduce a resolution prohibiting that couple on Knollwood Road from tying into the town's sewer system. Their request is on the Council agenda, and they're coming to ask permission to hook up to the sewer system. That couple really pissed me off last year when the husband wrote a letter to the editor criticizing the Council's budget. He never even called me."

Not to mention they had political election signs on their front lawn for the other party, Kurt thought.

"Let them spend their own money fixing their damn septic system," Mitchell concluded in a tone that left no doubt of his animosity toward the couple.

Kurt recognized the stubbornness in Mitchell's voice, but decided to reply anyway. "It may not be in the town's best interest to deny them access to the sewer line," Kurt offered carefully. "After all, they do have a problem and they have come to the Council for help. They could even file a suit against the town." *Darn, the irony of a Council member having his own personal agenda in deciding to give a hard time to a citizen, and for reasons that the citizen may never know about, the damn world of politics!*

"The hell with them, I'm going ahead with the resolution," Mitchell retorted angrily. "I'm only calling because I want you to have the health department report ready on their septic system, just in case I need it to show their septic system can still work. Leave it at my Council seat."

"No problem," Kurt replied. *Perhaps you also want a list of their campaign contributions.*

"I'll see you Monday. Have a great weekend." The line went dead, ending the conversation almost as abruptly as it had started.

Perplexed, Kurt stared at the phone still in his hand. *Another exciting meeting to look forward to. The citizens affected by the Council's vote on their sewer connection will probably never know that the resolution to deny them sewer access would have nothing to do with the merits of their case, but rather the pettiness and intent of one Council member to cause them grief. One Council member who's mad at them because of lawn signs and probably a political contribution to the opposing party, as well as the fact that they wrote a letter to the editor criticizing the Council on the budget.*

Kurt knew that Mitchell could be very persuasive with the rest of the Council with his determination and persistence. He would use the health department report, an independent analysis, which stated the septic system could still function. He was a good speaker, and could come across as very knowledgeable on town topics. Some Council members hardly read the information packets that were sent to them before each meeting. But not Mitchell. Unfortunately, he mused, *he reads everything.*

"Another happy call from Mitchell?" Liz interrupted Kurt's thoughts as she stood in the doorway.

"Ahh, yes, he's such a pleasure to talk to."

"You've not been his favorite person ever since you didn't hire his daughter for that recreation job last year," Liz offered.

"We had a professional review board interview her along with the other candidates. She bombed out," Kurt replied. "To people like Keith that doesn't matter. He sees himself as a very important Council member, and that should have counted. His daughter did not get the job, period."

"Don't confuse him with facts," Liz admonished with a wry grin.

"Politics, such fun," Kurt mused. "There is an expression among town managers, 'your friends come and go, but your enemies accumulate.'"

"Very true, Kurt, yes, very true."

"Anyway, I'll need the file on the Clark's septic system, the house on Knollwood Road."

"I'll get it ready. Did the shopping center come up?"

"Sure did. Mitchell wants that fiscal report sent to him before it's put on the agenda and becomes public. I reminded him it goes to all the Council members at the exact same time. "

"That's your standard procedure," Liz responded with a perplexed look on her face. "He knows that."

"He certainly is strongly in favor of the shopping center. And knowing him, he will push to get his own way. I could see him trying to influence the Commissioners, and even getting a few Council members to also call them. After all, the Council appoints them to the Commission, and some of their terms are coming up."

"You could be right." Liz said. "The shopping center has both good and bad points, and I know several of the Commissioners are on the fence, and last night's hearing didn't help matters. I've felt right along it was a good proposal, but now I'm not sure if I'm in favor of it. My husband and I have had several discussions on it."

"I agree. I sat through three long nights of hearings. I felt it was great for the town- more tax money, new jobs, a cleaning up of that overgrown area full of litter. It seemed like a homerun for the town-until the last two nights of the hearing. Those neighbors were angry, really angry. Now I am not so sure it will be the best thing. After listening to the arguments that were presented, I just don't know. Something just doesn't seem right about it, but I can't put my finger on it."

"Maybe because Mitchell is strongly in favor of it?" Liz asked in a teasing voice, knowing full well the conflict between Kurt and Mitchell.

"Cute."

Liz started to say something, but stopped as Kurt continued.

"This shopping center can bring in a lot of taxes, and this is an election year. It would be a good campaign issue, especially since taxes went up two percent last year. The councilors always try to avoid a tax increase in a local election year, the odd year, basic rule of politics. We seldom see tax increase in the local election years."

"Which means most likely no tax increase this year, " Liz added sarcastically.

"Going to be hard, that's for sure. Decreased state revenue, labor contracts, all are going to hurt the budget. However, they did build a cushion into the budget this past year with that tax increase. So, as you point out, it was an even calendar year, so no local elections."

"Politics—it stinks," Liz responded, rolling her eyes.

"But that is why this shopping center can be so important. It will build up the tax base. It will add to the tax rolls, and benefit the town overall."

"Except for the people living around the area. They won't be happy campers, that's for sure," Liz responded as she turned to search for the Knollwood Road file.

"True, but they are a small group. What will be interesting is if they continue to mobilize and develop political strength. They certainly came out strong at the hearings, surprised everyone, including me."

As Liz left, Kurt folded his hands and reviewed the project once again. Why was Mitchell so sure of the benefits of the shopping center? He wants this thing to fly right through the zoning process. He knows it takes time and all aspects have to be considered. He's usually the one that wants all the information on everything. Examine all facets, but not this one. *Curious. Very curious. Perhaps he has more of an interest in this than just that of just a Council member. Hmmm.*

Chapter 7
PZC CHAIRMAN AND REPORTER CONVERSATION

Thursday, February 28

Jim Bradley sat quietly in his kitchen trying to concentrate on an engineering report for his early morning meeting in his office. He turned down the TV volume on the 6:00 evening news and picked up his report for the meeting. He could not focus, his mind kept returning to the last three nights of the hearings on the shopping center. Having served as Chairman of the Planning and Zoning Commission for five years, he knew local hearings got ugly, but the intensity of these hearings bothered him, especially last night.

"You surely have something on your mind dear," his wife Ann said, breaking into his thoughts. "You seemed very distracted during dinner, and unless you are practicing reading upside down, I suggest you turn your report around," she continued with a grin.

Jim laughed and put the report down, first turning it right side up. "You're right Ann, my mind is not focusing right now." He turned to his wife, a petite woman who had seen her 50th birthday come and go. Having been married for over 25 years, he knew that she could read his moods, and as usual, she was right on. Gray streaks of hair blended with her long black hair, held in place by a head band that Jim often joked was the twin of the eye visor of Georgi La Forge on Star Trek.

"Must be town business— I recognize that faraway look. Wouldn't be your shopping center hearings by any chance?" Ann queried, knowing the answer. "Just because you spent the last three nights at the high school on those hearings and didn't get home before midnight is no excuse to make it four nights in a row. I am starting to feel like an afterthought, a fixture in the house. There is life outside of the town hall," she slowly added with a seductive smile.

"You're right, as usual," he smiled, picking up on her mood. "Actually I was really surprised by the intensity of the hearings, especially last night. I anticipated, or thought I did, the controversy this shopping center would generate. I surely underestimated the effect Attorney Burns would have in igniting the anger of the crowd. Her presentation set that crowd on fire, like a room was full of tinder and her closing remarks were the match."

"That's what Janet Johnson's' news article today said," Ann replied. "I knew last night when you came home you were upset. You tossed and turned all night and you ground your teeth. You only do that when you are really upset," Ann's voice turned serious. "Honey, is this volunteer job for the town really worth it?"

"Sometimes I wonder. For the most part I enjoy my service to the town," Jim placed his office report down on the table and looked directly at his wife. "It's a way of giving something back to this community. Covingford is such great place to live. But then you get projects like this that quickly become so controversial. People you thought you know so well suddenly are angry with you. They even stop talking to you. And all I am trying to do is stay neutral, make an informed decision, and run an organized meeting. It's so frustrating," Jim shook his head, half in disgust, have in amazement.

Jim and Ann had lived in Covingford for twenty years, and their children had gone through the local school system. They had many friends in town, mostly through people they met at their children's school sports and music programs. Jim, an engineer by education and training, was vice-president of his division at Pratt and Whitney Aircraft in Middletown. Approaching his 55th birthday, he maintained his six-foot lean physique by playing tennis three times a week during the winter months and a few rounds of golf each week in the warmer months. He had joined Pratt and Whitney after returning from a tour of four years with the Navy. A graduate of the University of Connecticut Engineering school, he eventually obtained his Professional Engineering license. The recent NCAA runs of the UCONN women's basketball championships made him even more proud of his undergraduate school, and he looked forward to the upcoming March madness games as a diversion from both his town position and his work obligations.

After graduation, he qualified for the Navy's Officer Candidate School in Newport, Rhode Island. Following graduation he spent the next three years on a destroyer. His education as an engineer, plus the leadership training in the Navy, provided him with an inner strength in dealing with controversy. He became known as a no-nonsense individual with a good sense of balance and fair play. His personal life reflected his stability, having recently celebrated his twenty-fifth anniversary. Jim and Ann had two children, both away at college, one in DC and the other in Boston.

"Public officials are always looked on with some skepticism," he continued. "A carryover from the Watergate scandal and the Nixon era, and now the shenanigans going on in Washington with firing of the FBI Director."

"Some skepticism? That's an understatement," Ann interjected. "I am sure there are a few people who think you get big bucks for chairing the Commission."

"You're right. It is amazing how often people comment on how much we are getting paid. Many people refuse to believe that the position is strictly volunteer, even when I tell them to their face. They look at me like I have a screw loose." He crossed his eyes, stuck his tongue out, and wagged his head.

Ann laughed. "I suggest next time the Town Council is ready to make appointments to the PZC, you submit those peoples' names for consideration, then let's see their reaction to this 'high paying' job," Ann said with a smirk. "Then they can have the opportunity to earn 'the big bucks.'"

"That would be fun to watch. However the reality is that most people just sit on the sidelines and criticize. They never step up to the plate. Democracy is not a spectator sport," Jim continued. "You know this shopping center proposal could be a real boom to the entire town – more employment, tax revenue, an attractive site in place of the run down, under-used, unsightly overgrown field and wooded area that it is. I had to laugh to myself when Attorney Burn called it a 'pristine open space.' Not quite pristine, but a few days of trash pick-up would do wonders for the area."

"Pristine open space, that is a laugh. But as you say, mostly litter and some trash," Ann added with a note of skepticism. She moved over to the side counter where she started to arrange a vase of flowers. "I can't wait till spring so I can go out and plant my own flowers instead of buying these cut ones. I did plant some bulbs last fall before the ground froze." Ann glanced at Jim, listening intently to Jim despite her nonchalant demeanor and her focus on her flowers. Noticing a dirty cup still in the sink, she finished arranging the flowers and put the cup in the dishwasher. She always kept an extremely tidy kitchen.

"A little more than a month and April will be here, some early planting time, especially after this winter," Jim continued. "The impact on the immediate neighborhood is a problem, a real problem for the residents. Their quiet neighborhood is threatened – increased traffic, noise pollution, more people– a concern over their real estate values. And then there is the potential impact on our local grocery store. The residents view this proposal as Hades itself. Attorneys are representing both sides. An organized citizens' group with a fiery attorney on one side, a well-financed developer who hired a well-known local attorney on the other. Plus, look at the cast of characters at the hearing, several political honchos. Not sure yet what their actual role is. And the rumors I hear floating around about them. This whole project could be a real donnybrook!"

"I also have heard a few stories, none very good," Ann replied. "I just don't know what, or who, to believe anymore." Ann moved back to the table, drying her hands on a towel, satisfied all the dishes were picked up and her flowers in order.

Jim continued. "There is money behind this project – real money. Pilgrim Industries has an option on the land which they will exercise if they get zoning approval for the project. Pilgrim itself is a major out-of-town development corporation with deep pockets. They specialize in coming into towns, getting options on vacant land, hiring a local attorney who then applies for a zone change on their behalf. The zone change would allow them to develop the vacant land, build their shopping center, get it up and running, and then sell everything, and move on with a tidy profit. Their modis-operandi is to also reach out to local 'king-pin' political honchos to help 'expedite' their proposal."

"People like the Gargano cousins, and then the Bomb himself?" Ann half said, half asked.

"Bingo, you got it."

"Sweet, government at its best," Ann added sarcastically.

"Sure is, and there is big money involved. The value of the land goes from almost nothing to high priced real estate, with lots of cash going around. A recipe for possible clandestine maneuvering. That is what is so bothersome. There are a lot of behind the scenes discussions and negotiations, which can sometimes get somewhat shady. All in all, it is a volatile mix. Look at the hearings. They got real ugly at the end, and could have even gotten physical. Fortunately the Town Manager arranged to have a police officer present. A uniformed officer always seems to have somewhat of a calming effect on a crowd. I will let Kurt know that I appreciated the officer. His presence was very helpful."

"You always said he had a good head on his shoulders," Ann said. "And, from what I hear, Jim, you did a great job of controlling the crowd. Really super." She put her arms around him. "My hero!"

"Thanks Ann," Jim smiled enjoying the warmth of the hug as his focus shifted away from the project. "Look at your arranged flowers on that kitchen window-so warm and cozy. The outside thermometer reads a chilly 29 degrees, but **with the wind, I bet there is a** wind chill of 15 degrees! Not a good time for flowers, but such is February. Did you know that we are already picking up almost three minutes of daylight a day? In another month the daylight hours will really be substantial, and by April, people's interests will turn to the outdoors. But for now," he continued, "indoor activity is the main focus, be it college basketball or for some, local politics – all are in full bloom."

"Whatever!" Ann responded with a little wiggle of her hips and a sly smile.

A broad smile lit up Jim's face. "Yes, whatever!"

"You don't have a meeting tonight, do you?" she asked coyly.

"No, home for the evening, no plans—yet!"

"Well let's just see what develops," She said with a smirk. "In the meantime, can't wait for March to come and go, it's such a dreary and miserable month. By April there are real signs of spring, but May is the month to plant. My Italian grandfather always warned me about planting before Memorial Day."

"Only real good thing about March around here is March madness, college NCAA and NIT finals," Jim offered.

"That's for sure. UCONN basketball, both men's and women's. The women's team is racking up so many NCAA championships. And what was it, both 2004 and 2014, when, both men's and women's team won the NCAA championships? The State went wild! I have never seen so many Huskie banners and bumper stickers. You even put one on your car! Certainly helps us get through these long winters."

"Yup, both were great years. UCONN has captured peoples' attention. A great sport. And look how many former UCONN stars played basketball for the USA at the 2016 Olympics! And another gold medal. Interestingly, there are people who also consider politics a sport, a blood sport. It becomes the focus of their lives. And now this shopping center has entered this arena. It is getting nasty, and I am afraid it will get worse. To tell the truth, Ann, I am worried, very worried, over the behavior of some of our town officials."

"Such as?"

"A few of our town council members, and especially a few of our PZC Commissioners. This shopping center proposal is so volatile with each side dug in. It's very possibly going to wind up in court. Any misstep or idle comment by a commission member will be blown out of proportion and used in any appeal, by either side. The lawyers will pounce on it."

"But this is Covingford, small town USA. Not a big city. Covingford has never had a scandal involving its local government-it's too small to be corrupt. Too many people watching every move," she added.

"You would think. But look at the embezzlement that has gone on in the small towns around the casinos in eastern Connecticut, local finance clerks, not high level. And who can forget the home-grown finance director who embezzled millions of dollars from his own town for years. Made headlines not only in the Inquirer, but statewide in the Hartford Courant. He grew up in town, everyone knew him, trusted him, local schools and all."

"Oh yeah, the one in that town just outside of Waterbury. As I recall, he also had a "cookie" on the side, and she turned out to be his downfall," she added with a broad grin.

"That's the one. The local board of education had to borrow money just to finance its payroll to get through its fiscal year. Not a pretty sight. And let's not forget about some of our big city mayors, in jail for corruption and bribery."

"And even our former State governor got in trouble. Disgraceful."

"No argument there. Throw in some of our legislators and you realize it can happen at any level. And in this proposal, the stakes for some reason seem to be higher than what they should be."

"Perhaps a hidden agenda?" Ann asked, a worried expression creeping across her face. "I think you are right, it may be time to remind your commissioners of the proper procedures that have to be followed now that the formal hearings are over."

"Good idea. This project will certainly test their mettle. I hope our newest commissioner, Jerry Katz, is up to it. He's still in his first term, although it is almost two years already. There's a lot of pressure on commissioners. Marilyn, Don and George have been on the Commission for several years, so they should be well seasoned. But Jerry, I don't know, this is his first real test. But best to talk to all of them. Yes, Ann, a very good idea."

The ringing of the phone interrupted their conversation. Jim walked over to the refrigerator and picked up the portable phone that was hung on the wall next to it. "Mr. Bradley, good evening. This is Janet Johnson from the Inquirer, hope I am not disturbing you."

"No, quite all right," Jim replied after a brief hesitation. He knew that as a public official he had to be accessible, and had often told the reporters he preferred calls in the evening rather than at his place of work. He looked up and caught a glimpse of a worried look on Ann's face as she mouthed "be careful."

"I need to flush out my story on the hearings with a few comments, so I will use anything you want to say," Janet continued.

"I can't appear prejudiced on the project, so I can't comment on its merits."

"I understand. How about a few comments on the procedures now that the hearings are over? There is such a tremendous interest in this proposal."

"Sure is. You seem to have an article on it in almost every edition."

"People want to know what's going on. Especially that neighborhood group. Everyone in Covingford is now watching this fight. Our local circulation has increased 25% since this project was proposed!"

Jim sensed the glee and enthusiasm in her voice. "Yes, there is a lot of interest in this one."

"The public wants to know, has a right to know, especially when it directly impacts their neighborhood. And this project is the biggest one in years in Covingford," Janet said.

"It's not going to be an easy decision."

"That's for sure. Can I quote you on that?"

"I thought you wanted a story on procedures- shall we stick to that please?" Jim asked with a slight irritation in his voice.

"Sorry," Janet replied, letting the rebuff slide. "What happens now that the hearings are over?"

"The Commission has 65 days from the close of the hearings to make a decision on the proposal. We will be discussing it at our next few meetings until we make a decision. But first we have to catch up on other old business. This proposal has put our other agenda items on the back burner."

"Can anyone speak on it at your meetings or submit another petition on the shopping center?"

"No, the hearings are closed. No further public input is allowed. The Commission will now hold public meetings, not public hearings, and the Commissioners will discuss the application. They cannot receive any further input on the proposal, not even a petition. Any petitions had to be submitted during the open hearings so the developers had a chance to reply. It is now up to the Commission to discuss, debate, and then vote at an open public meeting."

"What about the Town Council?"

"At this point, just the PZC votes. That is why the Town Council is very, very careful on whom they appoint to the Commission. It is a very powerful land use board."

"Can either side appeal the decision?"

"Yes. Either side can sue the Commission and take it to court. So we have to be very careful on how we handle it."

"Directly to court? No local Zoning Board of Appeals?"

"No. There is a ZBA, but they cannot hear appeal decisions made by the PZC. Their role is to grant relief when an existing zoning regulation causes hardships, such as the need for a variance on a side yard separating distance. So, directly to court."

"Wow," Janet said, "that makes for a powerful Planning and Zoning Commission. If it does go to court, couldn't that take years to get a decision?" Janet asked with an element of surprise in her voice, her pen scribbling notes.

"It might be heard within a year, but that would be fast. But you're correct. Time is money, and if the Commission turns it down, it could kill the project if the developers can't wait around for an appeal to the courts."

"And what would be their chances of winning a court appeal?"

"I can't comment on this specific case, it wouldn't be proper. But I will say that the courts are generally reluctant to overturn local land use boards. It does happen if there is a blatant disregard for the facts or major errors were committed in the processing. Normally courts leave local decisions intact. But, in court, one never knows." Jim said, thinking he best put that caveat in, just in case in the future the Commission lost a case. *And, I don't want my quote to come back and haunt me as the press has a tendency to do. Newspapers love to go back years into their articles and resurrect a quote that may not necessarily apply to the current situation.*

"Can we talk off the record?" Janet asked, lowering her voice.

Jim paused for a moment. If he did not talk off the record, he knew the reporter could miss an important angle or part of some background that could help explain the issues. If he did talk off the record, he would have to be very very careful. Fortunately, in the past, Janet had been trustworthy in what was said to her and how she reported her stories.

"Ok Janet, off the record, way off the record."

"Jim, there are a lot of stories flying around on the political influence on this project. Pilgrim Enterprises has a ton of money behind them, and a good track record in winning approval for their proposals. There's big money in this project. And interestingly, I keep bumping into the names of the Garganos and of course, Dominic Columbo. Have any of them contacted you on this project?"

"No. They know better." Jim said emphatically. He shuddered at the thought.

"How about the rest of the Commissioners?" Janet persisted.

"I don't know, but they better not. This is a small town, and everyone talks to everyone else, so who knows. I hope we don't start getting political pressure on this one, but I wouldn't be surprised. Politics seems to enter everything around here. Problem is you can't always see it. Sometimes it is just below the surface. It's amazing how often people have their own agendas on different proposals."

"Self-promoting agendas? " Janet offered.

"You got it. You've covered enough town meetings so I'm sure you have seen it many times."

"That's true," Janet replied. Numerous Council meetings flashed through her mind, several votes she never quite fully understood. "Although I follow the Council meetings, I am surprised sometimes on the way the councilors vote, like there is an agenda behind the published agenda."

"Like you implied, Janet, hidden agendas, and even conflicts of interest. The clandestine world of politics. It's not my style, which is why I don't register with either political party. I am an independent. I don't owe any favors."

"Interesting. Any thoughts or comments on your commissioners and their possible involvement in politics? After all, you all have to be appointed by the Town Council to be on the Commission."

"No comment - on or off the record on that one."

"Sorry. Just my natural reporter's curiosity. How about any influence from the Town Council on the Commission's vote?"

"That can happen." Jim admitted reluctantly as he got up and walked over to the kitchen window. Outside the brilliant full Snow Moon was crystal clear in the frigid air with its low humidity. The craters on the moon were very distinctive. *Probably I should have been an astronaut. Then I would only have had to deal with issues like space, strange worlds, meteors, fuel cells, and oxygen, anything but politics.* Turning back he continued, "They are the chief elected officials of the town, and they take their role seriously, sometimes too seriously." He returned to his seat and stretched out his legs on the other chair.

"I guess you never know where they might be coming from," Janet continued.

"That's true. They are contacted by everybody. Their names are always in the paper, and they do try and please their constituents, some more than others."

"Jim, I'd like to go back on the record for a few items to flush out my next story on the shopping center." Janet made a note to herself, 'back on the record.'

"OK. Shoot."

"Is it a simple majority vote of the five member Commission to approve the project?"

"Yes, Since we have five members, it will take three members to approve it. That is why there are odd numbers of members on these commissions, to avoid a tie vote."

"If it is approved, then what happens?"

"We publish a legal notice of our decision, and then any court appeal must be made within 15 days of the notice appearing in the paper."

"And if the appeal is not filed in that time frame?"

"Ball game is over. The courts are very strict on following exact procedures." Jim had been in court several times, and he was quite familiar with the process.

"When is your next meeting?"

"In about two weeks, on the 11th. Commissioners are exhausted. And at that meeting we will not be discussing the shopping center. We have a big backlog of applications because of all the attention to the shopping center. So the 11th will be devoted to just catching up."

"No shopping center discussion?"

"No discussion. I will announce that right at the start of the meeting." Jim took a deep breath and continued. "We will hold a special meeting later in the month just on the shopping center."

"One last question, Jim. At your next meeting, just to be sure, will you allow any more comment on the shopping center from the public or the developers, or either attorney?"

"No. The hearings are closed, Janet. At the special meeting later in March, the discussion will just among the Commission members and staff. We will have a dialogue with the Town Planner and Town Engineer since they are our staff. That's it. No more public input."

"Thanks Jim. That'll do it. You've been very helpful and I appreciate it. I'll certainly be at your next meeting, and," she added, "at the upcoming Council meeting."

"You and a lot of the neighbors. I expect a lot of people at our meeting," Jim offered. He knew the Commission would now be watched very closely. "It's not going to be a simple issue. An awful lot of interest in this one, perhaps too much."

"That's for sure. My papers are really selling. Covingford's circulation has jumped dramatically. It's great for our advertising, and I can put in for my overdue raise," Janet joked.

"Janet, let me ask you a question—off the record of course." Jim's voice suddenly was very serious.

Janet hesitated for a minute. She was the one usually asking question. "Go ahead, Jim. What is it?"

"You travel in a lot of circles. What do you hear about the developers on this project? Any local names popping up?"

"Funny you should ask that," Janet said in a conspiratory tone. She quickly flicked back a few pages on her notepad. "I have gotten unconfirmed information that the Garganos have a major stake in this project, both financially and also a promise for the construction contract if it gets approved."

"Full employment for their firm for two years, and that means lots of local hiring. I guessed that already," Jim replied. "They're in almost everything that comes before the Commission."

"This is different. I haven't verified it yet, but they are more than just the local contact. Supposedly they have a huge financial stake in this, in addition to the no bid construction award. This could be huge! Dominic's in on it too."

"He tries to be in on everything." Jim offered. He shook his head at the mention of Dominic; Jim's opinion of Dominic would not reach the first rung of an extension ladder.

"But, this one, my sources tell me, is that he is in the project well over 100Gs."

Jim said nothing while the implications of what Janet just said settled in. "He doesn't have that kind of money," Jim said slowly. "No way."

"You're right, he doesn't," Janet continued. "However, he supposedly has gambling debts well in excess of that amount, and that debt is being used as leverage against him to have him use his 'influence' to get the project approved."

"Oh Oh, that's trouble, big time. He's dangerous enough as it is, never mind when he has a major financial stake in a project," Jim exclaimed in a surprised voice. His mind raced as he digested the information on Dominic.

"He's such a lovable character," Janet replied sarcastically. "Too bad he is so kind to dogs – might be his only redeemable characteristic."

"You're right – maybe it's his only redeemable quality. Thanks for the info Janet. This project is big enough to bring all kinds of people out of the woodwork. I'll see you at our meeting." Jim hung up the phone and stood still for a few moments, lost in thought over Janet's bit of information on the Garganos and especially about Columbo.

"Trouble?" Ann asked as she quietly entered the kitchen. She knew the answer just from the look on her husband's face.

"Columbo again, he's such a pain in the ass. Plus the Garganos. What a combination. Columbo always acts as their henchman. Not the brightest star in the sky, but devious and very sly. Trouble is he may have a major financial stake in the shopping center, which will make him more dangerous than usual, much more dangerous. Damn."

Friday March 1
SHOPPING CENTER HAS LOCAL TIES-
LOCAL POLITICIANS INVOLVED?
By Janet Johnson
Inquirer Staff Reporter

COVINGFORD - The large shopping center proposed by Pilgrim Enterprises could have ties to local political figures. Dominic "The Bomb" Columbo, Chairman of the local Town Committee, declined comment on an inquiry from this paper as to whether he had direct financial ties. Reliable sources, however, indicate that he has a major financial stake in the proposal, although the extent of it has not been determined. Calls to Sal and Peter Gargano, also members of the same town committee, were not returned. The Gargano cousins, according to a source who did not want to be identified, have a major financial interest in the project. All three attended the public hearings this past week. The shopping center was the subject of heated zoning hearings, which went on for three nights. The last hearing went to after 11:00PM.

The shopping center is proposed to occupy 25 acres and have several small retail outlets in addition to a large anchor store. Numerous residents opposed the project, expressing concern over the impact on their neighborhood. Attorney Patricia Burns, hired by the neighborhood, has vowed to sue the Commission if it approves the project. The

Planning and Zoning Commission has closed the hearings and will be voting on the project sometime in the next 65 days.

PZC Chairman Jim Bradley declined comment on the merits of the proposal, stating it would be "improper for any Commission member to speak on the proposal outside of the Commission meeting." He indicated that the Commission will hold a meeting on March 11th just to catch up on old business and would not be discussing the shopping center. The Commission will hold a special meeting just on the shopping center later in March. "But, no further public comment on the shopping center will be allowed," he emphasized.

Mayor Powers commented that "although it could be beneficial to Covingford, it would impact the neighborhood. It's strictly a zoning matter at this time. We'll just have to wait and see how the PZC votes. Until they vote, there is nothing anyone can do. I'm sure they will act in the best interests of the town of Covingford."

Chapter 8
THE TOWN COUNCIL MEETING

Monday, March 4

Covingford's Town Hall could have been on a post card advertising old New England, although it was only built in the 1940's. It had traditional architectural lines composed of red brick, white trim, and a sharply pitched roof to shed the New England snow. Its four stately pillars and white shutters provided a pleasant contrast to the red brick, all offset by a small clock tower in the front. Unfortunately, the building configuration had not kept up with the office needs as the community grew, and several departments had to be housed in other buildings. Recent changes in the Federal disability laws had forced major improvements, including an elevator and handicap bathrooms, accommodations the original designers had not anticipated nor made provision for. The Council Chambers had proven over the years to be inadequate since only seventy-five residents at a time could attend a meeting. On more than one occasion, meetings had to be adjourned to the high school cafeteria to handle the overload.

The décor of the Council Chambers itself was quaint; the dark wood paneling reflecting the age of the building. In the front of the room were seven raised cushioned chairs situated around a half round table. Each seat had a microphone in front of it, which not only amplified the sound, but which also tied in directly to the recording devices that televised and video-taped all of the public meetings. The tapes were eventually filed with the Town Clerk, since they were part of the public record and the State Sunshine laws required that they be made available to any citizen who requested them. Few residents ever requested them. They seemed to be accessed more by the Councilors themselves, especially after a heated argument at the Council meeting. In watching the tapes, they not only relived the arguments, but were able to exactly quote the opposition, although usually just a key quote, regardless if it was out of context.

The center seat at the Council dais was reserved for the Mayor, who ran the meetings and normally controlled the tempo. Off to the side was a small table for the Town Manager and the Council clerk, who was responsible for recording the meetings and keeping the minutes. The Manager, who served as the day-to-day administrator of the town, did not vote with the Council. His position was frequently compared to the position of a school superintendent who works directly for the board of education. He or she is their chief administrative officer and does not vote with them., but administers the day-to-day affairs of the running the school district.

Fireproof maroon curtains covered the windows, contributing to the dark tone of the chambers. The incandescent lighting fixtures on the walls helped soften the mood of the room, and provided a welcome relief from the harshness of the overhead florescent lights. Photos of previous mayors hung on one side of the room, showing their names and years of office, a small token of recognition of their unpaid position as mayor. On the other side of the room were framed covers of the annual reports of the town.

"It is now 7:30, and I am hereby calling this meeting to order - please stand for the Pledge of Allegiance," Mayor Robert Powers announced in his best official sounding voice, a tone he had practiced and perfected over the years. His voice matched his 6'2" stature, and, as he admitted often to himself, his good looks. He had well-groomed brown hair, and at age 42, still maintained his athletic build. In his second term of office, he had become comfortable in his role of calling the meetings to order and running them fairly efficiently despite occasional derailment efforts by an irate citizen or members of the opposing party. Everyone stood for the pledge, which was immediately followed by roll call.

"I'll entertain a motion to accept the minutes of last month's February Council Meeting" Mayor Powers announced, continuing in his official tone. The motion to adopt was made and carried without discussion.

Mayor Powers looked out over the public in attendance, trying to determine what issues they might bring up. He spotted Janet Johnson in her usual seat near the rear, pencil and notebook in hand. He had come to realize that it was in this location she could take in not only the remarks of himself, the Councilors, and the public when they addressed the Council, but also the many side conversations of the citizens as they commented among themselves on the proceedings. He had read several of her articles over the years where she had quoted citizens' reactions and remarks about the Council members from her strategic location, remarks that often made him cringe as he read them in the harsh glare of the printed word.

"We are now at the citizen participation portion of the Council's agenda. Would anyone like to address the Council on any issue?" he asked, hoping there would be no disgruntled inquires.

"Yes sir, I would like to inquire about a drainage problem we are having in our neighborhood," replied a well-dressed woman in her late thirties. She half stood, not sure of the procedure to address the Council. However, the tone in her voice left no question that she was not happy with the town. "My neighbors are here with me to voice our concern over a serious problem we are having and. . .

"Please state your name and address for the record," the Mayor interrupted.

"I am Kathleen Ashley of 109 Kentwood Avenue. I am here tonight with several people from our area. We are concerned over the lack of maintenance on the drainage ditch that runs through the back of our houses. Every time it rains, the ditch overflows its banks and floods our backyards. This impacts our septic systems and it's dangerous for our children. The town has done nothing to help us. We want something done and we want it done now. We have called Town Hall but nothing is getting done," she said in a strident voice.

"Yeah, the Town's done nothing," a man seated next to Ms. Ashley chimed in, not bothering to mask his dismay with the town.

The Mayor turned to Kurt and spoke clearly into the microphone so as to be sure the public could hear him. "Mr. Manager, could you please respond to these complaints? Can we advise these people when their complaints will be taken care of? They will need a specific timetable as to when public works will address them."

Kurt leaned forward in his seat and turned on his microphone. Looking at the Mayor and then the citizen, and then back to the Mayor, he responded. "Mr. Mayor, although we are working in that area, it is unclear if the town has the responsibility to clean the swale." He briefly focused on the residents, and then continued. "This is an older subdivision, and the original developer just showed a brook on his original subdivision map. There are no drainage or maintenance easements on the map or in the land records. That's the immediate problem; there is no indication that the town has any responsibility to maintain and clean the brook."

"So who does?" The Mayor asked in an abrupt tone, not happy there was no immediate solution. Ms. Ashley shifted her weight from one foot to the other, listening carefully to the dialogue. The neighbors with her also listened intently. Janet buried her head in her notebook, a smile on her face.

"Frequently it's up to the homeowners themselves." Kurt continued. "Unfortunately many of the neighbors over the years complicated the problem by throwing leaves and grass clippings onto the bank, which restricted the flow of the brook." A slight mummer rose from the neighbors. "There's lots of these situations all over town, and we are just not equipped to handle them all. Many of them are private issues, although the town frequently is asked to intervene and correct the problem. We are not even keeping up with the drainage easements where we clearly have responsibilities."

"Well at least let's send a crew down to take care of the major debris," the Mayor continued, "and we will have to look further into this problem. I will also ask the Town Attorney to give us some direction on the Town's legal responsibility in this matter." Turning back to face the speaker, the Mayor continued in a sympathetic tone. "Thank you Ms. Ashley, for bringing it to our attention. Does anyone else wish to address the Council?" the Mayor asked in a louder voice, trying to move the discussion away from a problem that he realized the town could not simply solve.

"Yes Mr. Mayor" a man in his late 50's wearing a plaid shirt and worn jeans stood up, nervously twitching his hands. "My name is Jim Wells and my road, Sunrise Drive, is full of potholes. Last night I got a flat tire and a bent rim. It will cost me $425 to have it fixed, and I have the estimate right here to prove it." He rapidly waived a small slip of paper in his hand, convinced that he had absolute proof that the town was responsible. "I expect the Town to pay this bill. And I want to know when the town is going to pave this road. I'm a taxpayer. What do I get for my taxes?"

"We have a five year road program, and your road is on it," the Mayor immediately responded, almost sure that Sunrise Drive was on it. "I am not certain what year it is scheduled. Perhaps the Town Manager can answer." He looked directly at Kurt.

"Yes Mr. Mayor, it's scheduled for new drainage and paving in two years." Kurt responded.

"Two years! Two years! You gotta be kidding!" Jim Wells waved his receipt even higher over his head, convinced that it was absolute proof that the road had to be done now. "That road won't last for two more years. It keeps getting worse and worse." Turning to the citizens around him, he continued, "I bet if a Council member lived on that road it would get taken care of a lot sooner." Laughter erupted from the citizens seated around him. Janet let out a quiet laugh, her pen never stopped.

"You tell'em Jim," one of the men said in a loud encouraging voice.

"We do maintain a strict plan on our roads, *regardless* of who lives on them," the Mayor replied, the irritation in his voice quite clear. "However, I am asking the Town Manager to send a crew tomorrow to fill those potholes. Unfortunately we have several roads like this, especially after the January thaw. The freezing temperatures followed by a thaw, then refreezing and re-thawing, cause numerous potholes on our old roads. They just don't have the proper base underneath them." This brief overview of the cause of pothole problems had been used many times by the Mayor, and he was pleased with himself for knowing the process. "We'll see what we can do. Thank you for your comments," the Mayor concluded, brushing over the question of the cost for the wheel repairs. "Does anyone else wish to address the Council?"

"CITIZENS BLAST COUNCIL ON POTHOLES AND DRAINAGE" Janet scribbled on her notepad, looking for the headline grabber. Not a lot of substance for a strong story, she thought, but it will attract readers. Everyone hates potholes, and drainage problems are common enough to attract their interest. *Yes, this will create a lot of interest.*

"Mr. Mayor, I have a question for the Council." A young lady in her mid-thirties stood up. She was well dressed and her voice was firm. She immediately received all of the Councilors' attention, as well as the other citizens around her. "I attended the zoning hearings last week on the proposed shopping center, all three nights. Three long nights and. . .

"Please identify yourself for the record," the Mayor interrupted her, although he recognized her from the hearings.

"I am Suzanne Finch, 178 Hill Top Lane. My question is this. Why didn't any Council member, or you Mr. Mayor, speak at the hearing? This is a major issue for the Town. It has a major impact on our neighborhood. We were all out there, every night. And yet, we did not hear one elected official speak on the project. Where do you stand?"

"It's in the hands of the PZC," the Mayor quickly interjected. "They held the hearing and they are the ones who will vote."

"But you are our elected officials. We put you in office to guide our town. We have a right to know where you stand on important issues like this. After all," she persisted in a menacing tone, "when we vote in November, we have to have all the information on you so we can decide if we want to keep you in office."

The citizens seated in the audience all murmured their approval and nodded their heads. Several of the Councilors suddenly became uncomfortable and began shuffling their feet. They knew that Ms. Finch lived in the neighborhood that would be directly impacted and therefore must be against the project. Thanks to turnout at the hearings, newspaper articles, and letters to the editor, they were well aware of how quickly the neighborhood had organized and the number of people who had joined the ad hock anti-development movement.

"I'll make a comment," offered Councilor Mitchell. The other Councilors collectively breathed a sigh of relief that he had spoken up, thereby diverting attention from them on a hot topic. "This project has a lot of benefits for the Town- taxes, jobs, a cleaning up of a weed infested area that just collects litter. I think it will be good for the Town and we should support it. Nobody wants development in their backyard, but something has to be done with the land-and I think this is a good proposal."

"Have you visited our neighborhood?" demanded Ms. Finch. "Come on over and look at our streets and the number of children in our area. We don't need the extra traffic and the mess it's going to bring. Litter - you want to see litter? Go down to that shopping center outside of Middletown and look at the litter. Take a ride and open your eyes and . . .

"Please Ms. Finch," the Mayor interrupted. "This issue is in the hands of the Planning and Zoning Commission, and this is not the place to get into an argument. We will listen to any further comments you want to make, but we will not have a debate here."

"Elected officials – we put you in office and we can take you out," she threatened. "We will be watching you on this project - that's all I've got to say right now." She sat down, and the look on her face left no doubt of her feelings.

"There being no further comments," the Mayor continued, anxious to move away from this controversial topic, "the Council will now go to its regular agenda."

The pros and cons on each agenda issue were discussed, deliberated, and then acted on by the Council. As the meeting dragged on, the citizens in the audience quickly became bored until the Council reached the sewer request on the agenda.

"Do any of the residents here wish to be heard on this proposed sewer connection?" The Mayor asked, knowing this was a key topic for several in the audience. "This is your opportunity to speak."

A couple in their early forties slowly stood up. They look briefly at one another and then the husband started. "Thank you Mr. Mayor for the opportunity to speak," a touch of anxiety was clearly in his voice. "My name is Chris Clark, and this is my wife Marlene. This is the first time we've ever appeared before the Council and. . . and I'm a little nervous." He looked around at the citizens with him and they nodded, giving him the encouragement to continue with more confidence. "This sewer connection will save us a good deal of money and aggravation since we are having regular problems with our septic system. After each heavy rain, there is a real. . . Ah. . . fragrance in the air. . . " A hushed laugh and murmur greeted this comment. Everyone realized this was a serious problem.

"Please continue Mr. Clark," the mayor encouraged in a soothing voice.

"Our neighbors will grant us an easement to go across their property so we can tie into the town sewer system. Our alternatives are to pump sewage up a hill to the main line or repair our septic system. We got a high water table, which ain't good for septic systems. To pump up the hill will be expensive and will require regular maintenance. Plus, guess what happens when we lose electricity?"

Another round of laughter, somewhat louder.

"We need help. We're requesting permission to tie into our neighbor's line and then connect into the town's system. Our neighbors here," he gestured to the people sitting around him, "have agreed to allow us to do this. All we need is the town's approval." Mr. Clark stopped speaking and stood there, unsure of what else he was to say. He slowly sat down next to his wife.

"Thank you for your comments Mr. Clark. Anyone else have anything to say?"

"I'd like to endorse the senior citizens' request for the bus that. . ."

"Excuse me sir," the Mayor interrupted. "We are just taking comments now on this sewer request. We will address the seniors next on the agenda."

"Sorry. . . Sorry Mayor," the embarrassed senior citizen quietly sat down.

"The Council will now discuss Mr. Clark's request. Does any Councilor have any comments on this issue?" The Mayor asked as he looked around the table.

"Yes, I do," Mitchell responded. "Although I can appreciate Mr. Clark's problem, I have to speak against it." Mitchell's voice was intense. "It will require an easement across the property and this will create maintenance problems for the town in the future. If it breaks, the town will have to go in on private property. That could create problems. Our health department has confirmed their septic system can be repaired. I have their report here," waiving the report in front of everyone. "The more homes that tie into our limited sewer system, the more it will diminish our sewer capacity for economic development when we will really need it."

No one spoke. The room was as quiet as a graveyard at midnight as the impact of the Councilor's remarks sank in. Mr. Clark had a look of incomprehension on his face. Janet Johnson sat up, her interest peaked. *A little story? A little controversy?*

Mitchell smiled inwardly, knowing that he already had the votes to win his argument. His party had the majority control of the Council. They had met privately over the weekend to avoid the state open meeting laws which allowed members of the same party to meet without posting a notice. The members, following Mitchell's strong lead on the issue, acquiesced and agreed to a course of denial.

"I'm for granting permission to tie into our sewer system." Councilor Kathleen Corey suddenly jumped in. A member of the opposing and minority party, Kathy had learned the politics of the Council's maneuvers having served a few terms on the Council. "This man has a serious problem and he came to us, his town government, to seek our help. We should provide it to him. It's no big deal to allow him to hook up to our sewer system, and it will mean a lot to him. I don't understand your arguments and why *you* are against this," she looked sternly at Mitchell. "Is there something here I don't understand?" Her inflection left no doubt that she was really irritated at Mitchell's response. The audience sat mesmerized by the suddenness and intensity of the argument.

"It's easy to understand," Mitchell quickly replied in a sarcastic tone. "I want to save our sewer capacity for economic development, which will help our tax base. Mr. Clark's house can survive with a septic system, so why waste our sewer capacity. Let's save it for economic development. Look at the shopping center that wants to come in. It's important for our tax base, and we need to make sure we have adequate sewer capacity to handle it and any other big proposal that comes along. I don't want to waste our capacity - it is limited."

"The amount of flow his house will generate is minimum," Councilor Corey sharply retorted, her intense stare totally focused on Mitchell. Her tone left no doubt that she thought his argument was absurd. "One house is not going to hurt our sewer system. He needs help. Let's grant him his request and go on to more important issues facing the town."

"Don't tell me this isn't important!" Mitchell replied almost screaming into his microphone. The veins in his neck and forehead were suddenly pulsating. His face turned red with anger. The Council clerk just lowered her head and kept on taking the minutes. She had seen the friction between these two Council members before, usually along their individual party lines. Janet looked at both councilors, somewhat surprised at how quickly the debate had escalated. *Hmmm, is there something here more than a sewer connection? Mitchell seems to be very short fused these days when someone challenges him.* She made several question marks on her pad. *A citizen wronged by his government? Why turned down on a simple sewer line request??????????????*

"Enough, enough," Mayor Powers intervened, banging his gavel at the same time. Mr. Clark, is there anything else you want to add before I call for a vote?"

"Just that we really need this connection, and I don't understand Councilor Mitchell's opposition." His timid voice changed, it carried a tone of indignation to it.

Jumping in before Mitchell could reply and moving to control the situation, the Mayor announced, "Seeing no other discussion by the Council, would the secretary please call the roll on a motion to approve of the sewer connection for Mr. and Mrs. Clark?" The clerk called each Councilor's name for their vote on the motion to approve of the connection, following the established protocol of the Mayor first, followed by the Councilors in alphabetical order:

Mayor Powers - no
Councilor Baldo - no
Councilor Corey - yes
Councilor Jenkins- no
Councilor Gentile - "absent" announced the clerk for the
    record
Councilor Mariette-yes
Councilor Mitchell - no

"The motion to approve the connection fails, 4-2." the clerk announced, keeping her eyes lowered on her tally in front of her.

"The Council will now move onto the next item on the agenda." Mayor Powers immediately announced, anxious to move on right away.

"What! That's it! That's the end of it?" Clark asked in an incredulous voice, still standing with his mouth gaping open. He was a citizen wronged, a citizen who suddenly felt a great injustice. "I thought local government was to help people solve their problems, not increase them," his face flushed with outrage and surprise. "Who the hell does that Councilman think he is?" Lowering his voice he continued, "Wait till next election, I'll vote him out of office. That little bastard." Turning his back to the Council, he stormed out of the room, his wife running to keep up with him. Janet Johnson immediately jumped up and followed them out.

"Excuse me, Mr. Clark, my name is Janet Johnson, and I'm the reporter for the Inquirer." She held her notepad up almost touching his face, just in case he doubted she was a reporter.

He stopped abruptly. "I recognize your name."

"Thank you. I wrote down your remarks you just made. Do you really think the Council mistreated you? "

"Damn right!"

"Chris, watch your language. She's a reporter and every word you say will be in the paper tomorrow," his wife cautioned.

"I don't care. Who the hell do they think they are?"

"Why do you think Councilor Mitchell spoke against your proposal?" Janet asked, her pen scratching in every word.

"I don't know. I just don't know," Clark replied, his voice trembling half in anger, half in disgust. "I never met him before tonight. And the Councilors who voted with him. Pompous asses!"

"Really?" Janet asked in an encouraging voice.

"Chris!" His wife shouted, her face turning white.

"This Council just doesn't care for the average citizen unless he has political connections. I'm not gonna play that game." Chris turned to leave, his wife tugging at his sleeve.

"You said you will vote him out of office?" Janet inquired as she moved with him. "Are you going to campaign against him?"

"I'm going to make a pile of phone calls against him and let everyone know. He hasn't seen the last of me, that's for sure."

"Is there any final quote you would like to make for the paper?" Janet asked, pleased that she now had her lead story for the morning.

"Yeah. This Council has just made one taxpayer very angry for no reason." Sensing his chance for revenge, he continued. "I want the public to know how the average citizen is treated. These clowns are supposed to represent us, to help us." The fact that a newspaper reporter was writing down his every word suddenly made him feel better. *He'd get that Councilor and his cronies.*

"Thank you Mr. Clark. I have to get back into the meeting now. Sorry about your application." "Thanks." Turning to his trembling wife, he said in more gentle tone, "Come on honey, let's go home. We've wasted enough time here."

"*COUNCIL DENIES HOMEOWNER SEWER APPLICATION*"- *no, not strong enough for a headline* thought Janet. "*CITIZEN REFUSED RIGHT TO FLUSH INTO TOWN SEWERS*" – *hmm, better. I'll have to work on this once I finish the story itself.*

As Janet returned to the Council meeting, she heard the last few words of the Mayor's announcement. "Due to the lateness of the hour and the fact that we have one Councilor absent, we are postponing discussion of the trash contract, which will be a lengthy discussion. We will continue with the last two items on the agenda, the annual contract renewal for public health services, a routine item, and a request for town funds for a senior citizens' bus trip."

Councilor Mitchell half focused on the discussion, lost in thought on the vote that he had just won on denying the sewer connection. He inwardly gloated on his ability to control the Council with his party's majority. "The weekend meeting helped a lot," he mused to himself, "especially with the new Councilors who were just elected and don't really understand the way things work."

Mitchell's three terms on the Council had taught him the subtle ploys and tricks he could use to exert power and influence. He found the Council an interesting and important body to be on. It certainly was a break from the day-to-day issues he had to deal with in his paid job working for an import-export firm. On the Council he had developed a good deal of importance and influence. By hard work and persistence, he was able to carry out his ideas and opinions. He was even contacted on a regular basis by the Garganos on numerous issues before the

Council. Mitchell was pleased that they recognized his influence and importance on the Council. Most recently the focus was the proposed shopping center. He knew he had the ability to influence the Council, as well as the ability to keep an eye on the Town Manager and give him a hard time if need be to keep him in check. Yes, he thought, *the Town Manager is going to be held on a short lease on this one, or else!* The shopping center was a key proposal, and if he played his cards right, he could get the project approved. He might then even get a shot at being Mayor. If he really played all of his cards right, he could get rid of the Manager, or at least give him enough grief to force him out. With him out of the picture, his influence on the Council would be even greater. Yes, this shopping center is going to be very interesting indeed, with all kinds of side issues. *This could be the opportunity I've been waiting for.*

"We will now take up the last item on our agenda." The loud words of the Mayor snapped Mitchell out of his thoughts. "This is the request for an appropriation of monies for a group of our seniors who want to visit a power plant built into a mountain in Massachusetts." Although most of the citizens had gone home, a few senior citizens remained in the audience, waiting to see the outcome of the Council's decision on their trip. One elderly man was fascinated by the proceedings of the evening: the debates, the votes, and even the dialogues. It was his first Council meeting, and although he had come earlier to support his neighbor on his sewer request, he stayed to watch just how the Council would handle the bus trip request. Seated close to Janet Johnson who had quietly returned to her seat, he leaned over and asked "This is a popular item for us. Will anybody vote against it?"

Looking up from her notepad, she turned to the gentleman. "Usually the Council does not subsidize costs for these senior trips other than assigning a staff person to go along. But, we'll see. Never know what a Council will do," she winked with an all-knowing smile. A motion was made and seconded to approve an appropriation of $1,000 to 'help' the seniors with their bus trip. "Since there was no discussion, the clerk called each Councilor's name for their vote on the appropriation, following the established protocol of the Mayor first, followed by the Councilors in alphabetical order:

Mayor Powers - pass
Councilor Baldo - no
Councilor Corey - no
Councilor Jenkins- no
Councilor Gentile - "absent" announced the clerk for the
    record
Councilor Mariette-yes
Councilor Mitchell - yes

"Councilor Gentile is out of State," offered Councilor Corey, wanting to be sure she got into the record that her fellow party member was just not skipping the meeting.

"Yeah, sailing somewhere in the warm Caribbean while we're freezing here taking care of town business," snickered Mitchell. *Freezing our fuckin asses off.*

Corey let the sarcasm pass, but not without another dirty glance at Mitchell.

"I'd like to record my vote now" the Mayor suddenly said, ignoring Corey's explanation. "I vote yes."

"The motion to approve the appropriation fails on a tie vote, 3-3, with one person absent" announced the clerk.

"Holy smoke! It failed!" said the astonished senior. The others nodded in agreement.

"I'm not surprised," replied Janet as she recorded the vote.

"But the Mayor. Why did he pass and then vote yes at the end?" asked the senior. "I don't understand his vote. He passed when the clerk called for his vote, and then at the end he voted yes."

"It's a political vote," Janet replied. The grin on her face indicated that she had seen this before. "The Mayor knew the request would fail, but by waiting to the end, he could then vote for it and it would not change the outcome. He knew it shouldn't pass, but now when he appears before the senior citizens, he can brag that he voted for their project, but was outvoted by the rest of the Council. Meanwhile the public purse is protected in what would have been a bad precedent if it had gone through."

"What a wimpy way to vote," the citizen exclaimed, his head slowly shaking as he tried to understand this little window of politics that had just opened up before him. "Either you are for it or against it, that's the way to vote. That's the American way."

"Not always that way or that clean in politics," Janet whispered as she scribbled some notes down. *COUNCIL PUTS THE BRAKES ON SENIORS - hmm, I need a little more pizzazz, SEWERS AND BUS AXED BY COUNCIL, Better. NO BUS NO FLUSH. Not bad. I'll suggest that as a headline in the morning. I'll have to work on this one a little more.*

Turning back to the senior citizen she continued in a low voice, "You would be surprised at some of the antics that politicians will pull. Have to keep your eye on them you know. One of the reasons why I'm here at this hour, the eyes and ears of the public."

"Due to the lateness of the hour, and the fact that one councilor is absent," the Mayor was saying.

That's right, blame it on a councilor not in your political party, simmered Corey to herself.

". . . we will take up the trash contract at the next Council meeting. A motion to adjourn is in order," announced the Mayor, and it quickly passed. The Councilors left the meeting room, some more quickly than the others. A few lingered behind to further discuss the issues of the evening, although as soon as they looked outside and saw the heavy amount of snow falling, they quickly dispersed. The two lingering citizens also left, completely baffled by the night's proceedings.

"Politics" he complained to his friend as they stepped outside, "I'll never understand it. That agenda looked simple on the face of it, and yet, look at the votes. It seemed as though there was almost a second agenda, one not quite visible to outsiders like us."

"Hidden agendas," his friend offered.

"Not my cup of tea." The two continued to talk as they pulled up their collars on their overcoats and stepped outside.

"Look at this squall! New England winters, nothing like them—one surprise after another," the taller man commented.

"Just like the Council meeting," his friend quipped. They both laughed aloud, recognizing the truth of the statement.

Tuesday March 5
NO BUS - NO FLUSH
COUNCIL NIXES BOTH
By Janet Johnson
Inquirer Staff Reporter

———

COVINGFORD- The Town Council last night denied two separate citizen applications, angering several residents who were at the meeting. The first application was a request by Mr. Chris Clark of Knollwood Drive to hook up into the Town's sewer system instead of fixing his septic system. The vote led to a heated exchange between Councilors Mitchell and Corey, who supported the request. Councilor Mitchell led the vote against the hook-up, claiming it would take away from the Town's capacity which should focus on economic development. He cited the new shopping center as an example of needed sewer capacity. The motion to approve the request failed along party lines.

Following the vote on the sewers, Clark blasted the Council, stating, "They are insensitive to the needs of the Town's citizens. The public should know how these politicians treat us, especially Councilor Mitchell. The Council's denial will cost me several thousand dollars more to fix my septic system." Clark was particularity upset with Councilor Mitchell who spoke against his application. "It will use some of our sewer capacity which we need for economic development," Mitchell argued, swaying the Council's vote. "Pompous Asses" screamed an angry Clark as he stormed out of the meeting. "I'm not gonna let this drop," he threatened. "Mitchell will hear from me again."

The second vote was a request by the Seniors Group to underwrite the cost of a senior bus trip to Massachusetts. The appropriations vote for the senior bus trip tied at 3-3, and therefore the motion failed. Councilor Gentile is out of State. The argument centered around whether Town should get involved in providing a financial subsidy for a bus trip for a small group. A few seniors at the meeting expressed their dismay at the Council's vote. Mrs. McNamara of Bluebird Lane stated after the meeting, "Just wait till they are our age, and then see how they'll vote. No consideration for the elderly. At least the Mayor voted for our request, he understands. I'm going to tell all the seniors at the senior center how the Mayor supported us, but how certain Councilors voted against us. Here we are, senior citizens trying to live on a limited fixed income." Despite a request from Suzanne Finch for a statement on the Council's position on the proposed shopping center, the Mayor responded it was not their role to vote on it, but rather that it was a zoning matter.

The Council also addressed a number of other issues, including problems on potholes and drainage. The Town Manager was requested to check into these issues.

Chapter 9
THE CARIBBEAN

Tuesday, March 5

"The trick of sailing in the Caribbean is to rapidly adjust from sailing by charts, compass, and GPS, to sailing simply by straight line of sight, and keeping a close eye on the color of the water," Dave Gentile explained as he turned the large round wheel of the 36' Hunter sailboat, adjusting slightly to an imperceptible change in the wind. "The water colors help show water depth. And the closeness of the American and British Virgin Islands, combined with these perfect weather conditions, sets the stage for ease of sailing."

His sailing partner, Ron Barrieau, nodded in total agreement as he took a sip of his cold beer, gazing lazily at the little island off to the starboard side as he shifted slightly in his seat. "Yeah, it's tough down here—have to be a real pro at this. I'm glad I finally got the opportunity to come down with you to see for myself after all the stories you have told me over the years, " he replied with a smile on his face, partially shaded by the wide brim hat that he always wore when sailing. On more than one occasion his wife had pleaded with him to bury it in the trash before someone recognized him in it.

Dave just smiled and continued, "Like I told you before we came, it certainly is a far cry from the sailing skills we need when sailing along the coast of New England. We certainly have to know our exact position and destination in Long Island Sound. Remember the time we got caught in zero visibility in that freak summer storm?

"Yeah, that was hairy."

"Sure was! That fog bank rolled in on us as we sailed from the Connecticut shore to Block Island. Sun, then suddenly wind, rain, fog and limited visibility. Even the air changed from that clean salty fragrance to one of heavy storm conditions. Scary."

"I'd rather forget that trip!" Ron joked.

"And did you notice that there are very few navigational buoys down here?"

"Now that you mention it, I hadn't paid that much attention, been focused on the incredible azure water color contrasting with the sky, " Ron replied, nodding his head in agreement as he stretched out under the warm tropical sun, gently rubbing his uncharacteristic two-day growth of a beard that was poking through with slight hints of grey. "It's a rough world to get used to, that's for sure," he continued, slowly raising his beer for another sip.

Dave, again adjusting the helm, thought of the differences between these islands and home in Connecticut where he frequently sailed during the summer months on Long Island Sound. Here they were, in the beginning of March, relaxed and sailing on a chartered sailboat under a warm sun, cool breeze, and clear water - such a stark contrast to the icy conditions they had recently left at Hartford's Bradley International Airport. The fresh scent of the salt air filled his lungs and the slight coconut fragrance of the sun tan oil on his winter pale face added to his enjoyment. The small chop slapping off the boat's bow sent a light spray of mist over him, which, in combination with his sun tan oil heated by the Caribbean sun, completed his near euphoric state.

Ron pulled firmly on the halyard to tighten the sail. "I heard on the radio there was quite a snow storm last night back home. It was a real Alberta Clipper that blasted hard and fast right out of Canada. It really breaks me up that we missed it" he wryly commented. "And didn't you just miss a Council meeting?"

"Sure did, last night. Couldn't help it—choices to make," Dave said with a wide grin. "I'll call the Town Manager tonight and get an update. Agenda wasn't too heavy except for the trash contract, which got added at the last minute. But you never know what will come up at these meetings. So I missed a Council meeting and another snow storm, such is life!"

"Sounds like good timing to me," Ron added with a smirk.

"Well, the best planning in the world doesn't beat sheer dumb luck."

"That's for sure," Ron continued. "It's almost hard to visualize. The harshness of Connecticut's frigid winter storms with ice and snow, and here we are, riding up and down on these ocean rollers. Connecticut seems worlds away, in another dimension."

"Makes you wonder where reality is."

"Sure does!"

Dave and Ron were long-time friends and lived in neighboring towns. They had met in college, and now thirty years later, their friendship had continued as they pursued different careers. Dave had gone into the family roofing business, but continued his love for tennis by serving as the high school's tennis coach. Ron had joined the local phone company, and his passion for perfection combined with a keen mind and sense of fair play allowed him to rapidly move up in the management levels. Their diverse worlds always provided good topics for conversation, in addition to their many other common interests of friends, travel, and camping. Their wives, also close friends, were not able to make the trip due to the demands of their respective jobs, and their less than full commitment to the world of sailing.

"I had to laugh yesterday morning," Dave said, "when that sailing agent, Bud Rogers, reviewed the 'chart' that came with this boat. 'Not to be used for navigational purposes' was clearly printed on it. Rather ironic since they come with every chartered boat. These chartering companies don't want to keep up with the constant changes in sailing conditions, which would require the charts to be updated on a regular basis. And besides, as Bud pointed out, sailing from one island to another in clear visibility is pretty straight forward. Just keep our eyes on the color of the water and we won't even need a depth finder since these waters change color, turning lighter as they become shallower. Even our trip over to British Customs in Jost Van Dyke was easy."

"Which is why the charter companies prohibit night time sailing," Ron responded. "Not a bad idea at all, especially since there are many visitors down here, who, like us, don't know the waters."

Dave reflected back on the orientation session with Bud, the boat agent for the sailboat charter company. Bud had reviewed the local charts and carefully checked out the sailing experience of Dave the previous day. In his early forties, Bud had left the states to pursue a more leisurely style of life, taking advantage of his sailing knowledge and his natural ability to deal with people in a relaxed mode. Two years under the Caribbean sun had turned his slightly blond hair to a full blond, which blended in with his deep blue eyes and high cheek bones. The fact that he rarely did anything to his hair other than to run a comb through it, further added to his casual and laid back appearance. Dave quickly realized that

Bud's demeanor masked his seriousness and expertise in evaluating people who chartered from his firm. Underneath Bud's casual demeanor was a man who could quickly measure up the people he was checking out on the sailboat and evaluate if they really had the necessary knowledge and experience to safely charter the boat.

Dave had laughed to himself as he had watched Bud come to work that morning by his usual method of transportation, a 12' row boat with the bow weighted down by his Golden Retriever "Dockside." Dockside, faithful in his duty to accompany his master to work, was stretched out in the bow with his head resting lazily on the gunwales of the boat. As Bud left the rowboat to climb up on the dock, the Retriever lifted his head and gazed after him, thereby completing his first morning assignment of insuring that his master had arrived safely at work. This task completed, he then stretched out to soak up the warm winter sun, focusing on his next job, that of carefully guarding his master's row boat.

Dave had been standing on the end of the dock at the time. He had witnessed this entire ritual with a broad smile on his pale face. *Not a bad way of life*, he mused. It sure beats the commute in Connecticut this time of the year, fighting the traffic on I-91 just south of Hartford with its constant construction and frequent snow and ice storms; bumper to bumper traffic traveling either at 70 mph or crawling along at 5 mph-what a drive! *Something to be said for the row boat commute!*

As Dave and Ron sailed around the tip of Virgin Gorda, their conversation bounced back and forth over a number of items. Adjusting for a slight change in the wind, Dave commented "when we go ashore tonight at the Bitter End Yacht Club, I'll call Kurt for the update. I told him I would call. I am also curious if there is anything new on the shopping center proposal."

"From the newspaper articles and letters to the editor, that's sure a hot button right now," commented Ron.

"Sure is, and it's going to get hotter. Problem is we have a few Councilors who are less than honest when it comes to dealing with the Town Manager and with other Councilors. It's not what they say, but rather, what they don't say, especially when they seem to have a good deal of knowledge about what is going on."

"You mean some politicians are not totally honest? Wow!" Ron grinned.

"Cute. The new shopping center proposal is a good example of this. It's a major proposal and it will have a long term impact on the town. The hearings just finished and they were quite lively. People got really riled up, especially that one neighborhood group since the proposal is right in their own backyard."

"I've seen people get downright nasty when their neighborhood is threatened."

"They even hired their own attorney, and she made quite a presentation," Dave continued, his eyes scanning the billowing sails and the clear blue waters. "She really churned the waters."

"How does it affect you?" Ron asked. "You're on the Town Council. Isn't the proposal before your Commission?"

"Yup, it's their baby, at least for now. The center is big enough to require the approval of a few town boards and commissions, although the PZC has the largest and most important say in the proposal. They can make or break it. If they deny it, the proposal is DOA. If approved, then the Council and others will get involved. Even the political town committees are having an ongoing dialogue about it, and there are some heavy hitters on those committees."

"Unelected officials," Ron commented wryly.

"And they do influence public policy in the background," Dave continued. "The ones I am concerned about, however, really concerned about, are the Commissioners. They are under a lot of pressure right now—the heat at the hearings, the letters to the editors, lawn signs, and I bet they are getting 'advice' wherever they go in town. And they are not even paid, just volunteers."

"Such fun to be a volunteer," Ron said with a touch of sarcasm.

"I remember Pete Moore, the former town manager, the one just before Kurt," Dave said. "He told me that he could not even shop in town. People seem to think you're on the clock 24/7. One time he was getting a haircut and an irate citizen started verbally hammering him on a town issue. He was stuck in the chair, the barber right behind him with his scissors and comb, staring agape at the man. Pete finally had to get up, pay the barber, and leave."

"Haircut unfinished?" Ron asked, his mouth wide open reflecting his surprise.

"Yup, and it was a Saturday to boot!" Dave said wryly.

"Wow, and he was an experienced public official."

"Yes he was, and a good one at that. That's the type of verbal abuse that public officials often have to put up with. So when you have citizen volunteers, like the PZC Commissioners, who suddenly are faced with a hot potato like the shopping center, no telling what pressure they might be coming under."

"I bet they get phone calls we never hear about," Ron replied.

"I agree. And that's what I get concerned about. It takes years on a board or commission to get used to the pressure and abuse that one can be subjected to," Dave said. "I have been on the Council for almost ten years, and I've seen a lot. I know the phone calls I have gotten over the years on various hot topics - and this shopping center is as hot as these topics get," he added, a note of concern in his voice.

"How you put up with the BS and politics is beyond me," Ron replied. "I just don't have the patience for some of the malarkey that goes on. Meeting after meeting, phone calls-all that talk would just drive me crazy."

"Some people just like to hear themselves talk."

"It's bad enough I have to put up with it at the phone company with all of our meetings, never mind going to a bunch of night meetings and listening to all the nonsense," Ron replied. "I've got more important things to do. That's why I'll never run for elective office."

"You would be good on your Town Council," Dave quickly responded. "Part of the problem is that many citizens don't have a political agenda, and like yourself, just can't be bothered to spend the time to get involved. As a result, we often wind up with some people on boards and commissions who only have an ax to grind or just enjoy the feeling of power they get in controlling situations. Over time they develop their own personal agenda, which often is not in the best interest of the town."

"I still find it amazing the discussions that go on and on, even for something as common as trash collection," commented Ron. "Who would ever guess that trash could generate so much interest and debate? It certainly is not a sexy topic, but it never ceases to amaze me how much newspaper coverage is given to the topic. I put my trash out every week, and I don't think twice about it, unless they fail to pick it up or until they decide to play horseshoes with my trash barrels. Then I call Town Hall," Ron said with a wink.

"Having served on the Town Council for all these years, I now have a different appreciation for what is real and not real in municipal service," Dave replied. "Trash collection is one of the most visible services provided by local government. Not everyone has children in the school system. Most people do not use the police or fire services, and unless you are putting on an addition, you don't deal with the zoning agent or the building official. Add to this group those individuals who live on the State roads in town, and voila, they don't even get town-provided snow plowing."

"For taxpayers, trash is the tie that binds, so to speak," Ron slipped in, laughing at his own wit.

A slight shift in the wind caused Dave to tighten up on the sails, taking a better advantage of the wind's angle to the boat's direction. The small chop, in addition to the larger ocean rollers, further added to the relaxed mood and the conversation. The Hunter sailboat sliced through the troughs, its sleek lines cutting through the water like a hot knife through butter. The breeze maintained its constant flow, its direction varying by only a few degrees every now and then. The quiet moments lingered on as Ron absorbed the beauty around him. During the morning he had seen the most beautiful small island with brilliant white sand and just a few palm trees- it seemed to beckon to him.

Both Dave and Ron remained quiet, soaking in the breeze, the slap of the waves on the bow, and the fluttering of the sails. Breaking the solitude, Dave exclaimed, "This is the life. It certainly is different from sailing on Long Island Sound, where one minute you have a strong breeze and the next, you are wing-on-wing, trying to eke out every drop of breeze that may come your way. Here the breezes are more constant and don't move around the compass as much."

Ron nodded in agreement. "And you don't seem to have the sudden weather changes here that the Sound has."

"True, very true." Dave thought for a moment about sailing contrasts between Long Island Sound and the Caribbean, and then returned to thoughts on trash and municipal services. *How ironic. Here we are in one of the most beautiful settings in the world, and we're discussing politics and trash—sometimes they are one and the same.*

"Look at those clouds, the sky, our sails. Even the cattails on the sails are fluttering away in this breeze."

"Doesn't get any better," Ron murmured as they approached the harbor entrance.

"When we moor at the Yacht Club," Dave continued, "you'll even see trash collection taking place right in the harbor. There's a small open boat that comes around to each of the yachts and sailboats and takes bagged trash for a few dollars per bag."

"A local touch to a universal problem," Ron laughed.

"I think you'll like the Bitter End," Dave commented. "It's renowned throughout the Caribbean and has been rated one of the top tropical resorts. It offers a safe harbor, bungalows for rent, sailboats for charter, and great ambiance. Dining is excellent, which we will try tonight in the Clubhouse."

"Let's get serious here. How's the bar?"

"Great. Wait till you try one of their rum drinks. It fits this gorgeous setting."

"Alllllll right!"

"Fortunately we have a reservation for a mooring in the harbor," Dave continued. "So we will sleep a little more soundly tonight. There is also a water taxi service available to us, so we don't have to use the dingy."

Approaching the harbor entrance, Ron observed, "Sure is a large number of boats in here already, bet it's going to be filled by sunset."

"A busy place, certainly is a variety of boats - yachts, sailboats, trawlers, all sizes and shapes," Dave replied. "When we go ashore you can look around while I call the Town Manager. I'll just be a few minutes."

"Such a sacrifice you've made to be here. Maybe they didn't even notice that you were missing from last night's Council meeting," Ron said grinning even wider.

"Smart ass!"

Arriving on shore, Dave dialed his cell phone. After a few rings, he was glad to hear Kurt answer the phone, realizing the secretary had already left for the day. "Hi Kurt, Dave here, calling from the tropical paradise. How is it going?"

Kurt laughed. "Not bad Dave, but I am sure it is not comparable to what you are experiencing at this moment. I'm looking out the window right now and the thermometer is reading 29 degrees. Add in the March wind and I bet the wind chill is closer to 15 degrees. A bit chilly. What's the temperature down there?

"It's cooling off, almost down to 82, with a light breeze out of the west," responded Dave, as he smiled and gazed out over the harbor with its bright contrast of white yachts, blue water, and reddish sky. "Sunset in another two hours or so. May even have to break out a sweater later on, but we'll cope."

"I'm sure you'll put up with the hardship. You missed a surprise snow squall last night, a real Clipper. It left four inches of that white powdery stuff on the ground, just enough to make driving slippery again. Fortunately, we are at the end of winter, so people are acclimated to driving in snow. Unfortunately, last night's storm came before our weekly trash pickup, so barrels were all over the roads this morning from the snow plowing. You can imagine what my first dozens calls were about. Some people were truly convinced that our snow plow drivers used their barrels as targets!"

"Amazing. I know just what you're saying, Kurt. But just to keep things in perspective, we had to struggle with stiff breezes all afternoon, even got a little wet with the ocean spray, but we suffered through it. Right now we're at the Bitter End Yacht Club, and have to make some tough decisions shortly on what to have for dinner after cocktail hour."

"Tough life, Dave. Sure you're coming back? We do have a few more mundane issues here, but nothing like the life-threatening decisions you are facing," Kurt said in a bantering tone.

Dave could picture the wide grin on Kurt's face with the last comment, as well as the weather conditions Kurt had just described. "I did want to check on the trash contract and on the shopping center proposal. Any discussion or action at last night's Council meeting on either one?"

"No action. The trash contract was postponed to the next meeting. Just as well. Gives me more time to review the bids, and you the opportunity to vote on your favorite topic," Kurt said with a note of glee in his voice. "We received four bids, including the incumbent. This was three more than the last time we went out to bid. I think that's a result of the FBI investigation into the issue of collusion among trash dealers on what territories they would bid. I did advise the Council that the Public Works Director and I are still evaluating the bids. The issue is complicated by the fact that the local firm, Trash-a-Long, submitted a bid for the first time, and, at first review, it is the apparent low bid."

"Are they qualified? Their experience is quite limited."

"We are checking references. That's why we specify the 'lowest qualified bidder' in our bid specs. They do pick up at several private businesses and a few apartment residences out of town. Problem is I am already getting hints from Councilors reminding me that they are the local business who pays taxes, and the other firms don't. The second low bidder is a national firm with a good reputation and substantial experience. Since the bid results were in the paper three days ago, we are also receiving phone calls and letters from people asking us to go with the local firm."

"All unsolicited I'm sure," Dave commented drily.

"Absolutely-people just cheering for the local boy," Kurt replied. "I expect the review to be completed in another day or two, and then I can make a recommendation to the entire Council, just in time for when you come home."

"Thanks! What's the latest on the shopping center? We both spent lots of hours at the hearings and they were quite lively, to say the least. I also picked up some funny vibrations just before I left to come down here. It's a hot topic."

"Sure is," Kurt said. "The Mayor brushed it off, saying it was a zoning issue, not a Council issue. And the PZC has taken the week off after their marathon public hearings last week. They meet again next week on the 11th."

"They certainly deserve the time off, after all, they are all volunteers. As for the Mayor, he can be a little wimpy at times."

"A few citizens were not happy with him nor the Council members. They wanted to know where their elected officials stood."

"Understandable."

"Only Mitchell spoke up in favor of it."

"Not surprised. He has been strongly in favor of it from the get-go. Fortunately it's up to the PZC, not the public, nor the Council," Dave added. "And based on the reaction at that last night of the hearings, if this project was decided by popular vote of the public, it would have gone down to a flaming defeat. But there are two sides of the argument, as witnessed by the steady stream of letters to the editor in the paper, both for and against it."

"You're right Dave. It's going to be a tough decision. There are strong arguments on both sides. It's too early to tell which way it is going to go. Janet Johnson has called me several times on different stories she is doing on it, and based on her questions, she is doing her homework. I am always amazed by the amount of background information she can generate on a story."

"She's known for that. Makes a lot of people uncomfortable."

"She's got connections, and knows how to get people to talk, especially off the record," Kurt added. *She sure does.* "I am sure there is a good amount of behind the scenes maneuvering on this one-certain names keep popping up. It's going to be interesting."

"You're right," Dave said. "I also heard some names associated with this project. There are a few heavy hitters on this one. I keep hearing the Garganos' names, along with our friend Dominic. He always seems to be in the background of major proposals. Hope Janet is able to dig around and see what his connection to the project is. She does have that knack for getting to the heart of things."

"From the questions and comments she recently made to me," Kurt continued, "I expect more news articles shortly and she is going to be naming names."

"Interesting," replied Dave. "Anything else happen at the Council meeting last night that I should know about?"

"The Council denied the request of a Chris Cark for a sewer hookup, it went down along party lines."

"What!! Why? That was a simple request," said Dave. "I know him. He sometimes gets involved at election time, but other than that, he rarely gets involved in politics or town affairs, or asks for anything, so he must have a real problem."

"I think so. It was a request for a simple sewer connection to avoid having to stay on a septic system. Mitchell had his votes lined up before the meeting. Mr. Clark never realized that the debate on the floor was not what it appeared to be. Mitchell had called me before the meeting and said he was going to move to turn it down since the guy had a campaign sign on his front lawn –for the other political party. Of course, that never came up, just some other reasons."

"Some people just can't come right out and say what is on their mind," Dave added.

"Also had an interesting vote on the senior citizen trip to Massachusetts. It wasn't a good idea to even bring the request before the Council, but Councilor Mitchell wanted to look good with the seniors, so he had it put on the agenda. Guess how the Mayor voted?"

"I bet he passed on the first count and then voted for it after it was clear that the motion had failed."

"Bingo. Exactly correct. How did you ever guess?"

"A favorite trick of his on popular but unfeasible votes," Dave said. "He doesn't do it often, but once it's done, you never forget it. A true political move."

"Ahh, the murky word of politics," Kurt sighed.

"Well, my cocktail partner is waiting, and we have a dinner table reserved which looks out over the harbor, so, I have to run. I expect to be back in Connecticut Sunday night, barring unforeseen circumstances. Tomorrow Ron and I are sailing down the channel, and plan to spend overnight in a protected cove off Norman Island. I hear there is even a pirate's ship there which is a floating bar and restaurant."

"Norman Island? Isn't that the island that was the basis for the book Treasure Island?"

"Yes, Robert Lewis Stevenson used it as his model for that adventure. After visiting it and checking out the restaurant, I will let you know how it is. After that, back to Connecticut."

"Enjoy the rest of your trip," Kurt responded. "Watch out for the Pina Coladas down there. They are so good, and with fresh fruit and local rum, they go down smoothly, too smoothly."

"I hear you. And, by the way, watch your back on these issues," Dave cautioned. "Some people in Town are not your biggest fans, and they would love to get rid of you if you get in the way of one of their pet projects, and believe me, the shopping center right now is somebody's pet. Take your choice of whom, there are several choices. And I don't have to remind you that Mitchell would love to have your scalp. I am convinced he is pushing to be Mayor, although he has never come right out and said it."

"Understood. I'll try and walk the line on this one," Kurt replied, not realizing just how tight the line was going to be. But as he hung up the phone, a funny chill came over him, as though someone had just opened the window and let in the frigid March air. "Strange," he said to no one but himself, "very strange feeling."

March 5
Letters to the Editor
The Inquirer

Hoity-Toity to the Toitee

The proposal by Pilgrim Enterprises to build a shopping center in Covingford is an abomination! It will destroy our town, ruin local businesses, bring increased pollution and traffic. Hoity-Toity, the up-scale anchor store, is too hoity-toity for us, go to the toitee, go back South. Leave Covingford alone. Get out of our town. PZC Commissioners vote NO!

Paul Burns
Covingford Resident

Where is the Mayor?

Something stinks in Covingford. A group of developers are trying to push a major shopping center on the town. These fat cats are just out to make a buck and don't give a darn about our town. This proposal will change Covingford's character and bring in all kinds of traffic and people. And where is our mayor? He is awful silent about this major proposal. Does he have ties to it we don't know about? What is his role with the Planning and Zoning Commission? It's time the citizens of our town demand answers.

Ralph Cavallero
Covingford Resident

Chapter 10
THE RESTAURANT DEAL

Tuesday, March 5

Dominic Colombo sat quietly with his back to the restaurant wall, preoccupied with the food he was devouring. He furtively glanced around the room, his eyes darting from one place to another, finally focusing on the three men he was dining with. The men with him were deeply engrossed in conversation, seemingly ignoring him. The Bomb heard every word despite their low tones and his grunts which moved in union with his jaws. All seemed to move in perfect coordination with his hands as he swept up the garlic balls and the olives. Occasionally he let out a louder grunt to indicate his concurrence with what was being discussed. His three companions carried on their conversation in subdued tones, despite the fact that their table was in the far quiet corner of the restaurant. They wanted no chance of their conversation being overheard. Their selection of the Tuscany Spa restaurant in the southern end of Hartford fit the bill perfectly-privacy, great food, and only a few miles from Covingford's Town Hall.

Dominic knew this place well. Located on Franklin Avenue, the Tuscany Spa was known for its bread balls laced with fresh garlic, large green olives dripping with spices and garlic chunks, strong Chianti wine in straw caskets, and a Tuscan menu. It not only was Dominic's favorite restaurant, but it was the favorite watering hole for many of Covingford politicians -great Italian food and a short commute. The Tuscany Spa also saw its share of Hartford's political clientele. Here was the place where deals were struck, issues hammered out, compromises reached. On almost any day of the week a member of a town board or commission could be found enjoying the gastro delights while engaged in deep conversations. Many jokingly referred to it as the "Town Hall Annex," in reality a moniker not far from the truth.

The lighting in the dining rooms was subdued, adding to its Mediterranean atmosphere. Pictures of Tuscany in central Italy hung on the wall, enclosed in elaborate gold frames. The aroma of fresh garlic - roasted, sautéed, and minced - permeated the restaurant. Outside, pedestrians would stop and sniff as the garlic fragrance drifted to the street, pushed from the rooftops by the kitchen vents, which was in effect, subtle advertising. A powerful invitation to come in, an attraction not unlike Homer's Sirens in Greek mythology that lured passing sailors to come ashore with their sweet singing. Inside the food was superb, the wine so warming, and often, oh so often, the political discussions extraordinaire.

Small tables and booths, discreetly separated from one another, allowed private conversations. More than one public issue involving Covingford had been discussed and decisions agreed upon over the years at these tables, and then washed down and sealed with one or more bottles of Chianti. Decisions were made, deals shook on, people introduced to others as networking took place. It truly earned its reputation as the Town Hall Annex.

Sal and Peter Gargano sat facing each other, Town Council member Keith Mitchell wedged between them, and much to Keith's dismay, directly opposite Dominic. Their table was set just for the four of them, with its white table cloth and single red rose in a thin vase. Mitchell tried to avoid looking at Dominic whom he noticed was already on his second basket of hot bread and dripping garlic balls. Images of a super powered Hoover vacuum cleaner hard at work flashed through Keith's mind.

"I'm doing my part to help get this damn shopping center through," Mitchell stressed, his voice barely above a whisper. "Despite all that opposition at the hearings, it actually looks like a good deal for the town." Sal and Peter leaned across the table as they listened intently, vainly trying to drown out Dominic's grunts as he spread butter on both sides of the crusty Italian bread. A broad grin enveloped his face as he focused on the hot bread, trying to decide if the butter had melted enough or should he just focus on the garlic balls while he waited. Mitchell wondered how one person could take such glee in eating. He glanced left and right, trying to avoid looking at the human garbage disposal directly opposite him.

"You're right Keith. This is good for the town, and it is big, really big," Peter said as he sipped his glass of the strong Chianti wine. "It will be a big benefit. An increase in tax revenue, new jobs, cleaning up of a run-down area— it's just what Covingford needs, despite what those jerks from the neighborhood said at the hearings. " He focused on Sal and Keith, both listening intently. Out of the corner of his eye he saw Dominic signaling the waiter for another basket of the garlic balls. Dominic's half loosened tie already had several new spots on it, and his shirt was rapidly catching up.

"There are other people in the state who are also quite interested," Sal added, finishing his cousin's thoughts. "Important people, with lots of money to invest. And there's big money in this project. . . and big political connections. Several large donations have already been made to our political party, to help, shall we say, facilitate the approval process."

"Yeah," inserted Peter in a perfect flow to finish his brother's thoughts, "kinda like an insurance policy, to help with any environmental reviews the state might get involved in."

"Great garlic balls," snorted Dominic as he reached into the basket and grabbed the last one with his short fat fingers. "Yeah, this shopping center will be a real plus, real good for Covingford, not a question in my mind. Boy, look at this garlic ball, so good, just dripping with garlic. No question, my favorite restaurant." Sal and Peter exchanged glances, amazed how Dominic could mingle the shopping center and the garlic balls without a break in thought. "I think every restaurant is your favorite restaurant," Peter quipped.

"We have some serious problems Dominic," Sal cautioned. "That neighborhood group with their pain-in-the-ass attorney really stirred up the crowd at the hearings. And now we have those damn lawn signs screaming 'Vote No –Save Covingford,' popping up all over the place. I've seen several throughout town, but especially in the neighborhood next to the proposed site. I've even seen postings on Facebook. Damn, they've acted fast, too fast."

"That is putting a lot of pressure on the Zoning Commission," Peter agreed. They could even turn it down. They need to have lots of discussion before they vote. According to this morning's paper, they'll have a special meeting in two weeks on March 18, just on the shopping center proposal itself, nothing else will be on the agenda. And another damn letter to the editor."

"I didn't get to see the paper yet. Did Johnson say anything else on the proposal?" Mitchell asked.

"Not too much. The next Commission meeting on the 11th is to catch up on other issues before them. The Chairman has said right along that they wouldn't allow any more public discussion on the project since the public hearings are closed. There will be a lot of residents from the neighborhood at the next meeting, just to show the flag and keep pressure on the Commission."

"And that does bring pressure—a whole audience of irate citizens, and they can't speak." Keith said.

"Interesting process this democracy," said Sal ironically.

"That's normal," Mitchell offered. "They usually hold a special meeting on any big project and this certainly fits the bill. The special meeting generally will just have the one item on the agenda. But, in the meantime, all these jerks against the proposal will go to every meeting just to keep the pressure on the Commission."

"Janet did throw in a comment about all the signs popping up all over town, both against and in favor."

"That's our people. We put the word out that we also needed letters in favor," whispered Peter. "It's a hot topic. Her article did review the procedures the Commission has to follow."

"But in the meantime, there are other minefields," Peter added, lowering his voice even further.

"Like what?" The Bomb asked in between belches. His attention shifted from the garlic balls to Peter, who winced as he watched the garlic juice drip down Dominic's pudgy chin.

"That pain in-the-ass reporter, Miss up-yours Janet Johnson. She's asking a lot of questions," Peter replied in a disgusted tone.

"Stupid bitch. She's always causing problems," Sal interjected. "Dom, did you see her brief article on next week's meeting?"

"Sure did," said the Bomb. "Looks like the Commission will do dittley shit at that meeting, mostly routine stuff."

"Yeah, the hearings really backed them up," explained Sal. "But I still am worried about Janet, she is always asking questions."

"Miss Ass-Hole Snoopy," Dominic added, also making no attempt to conceal his dislike for the reporter. "Only real nice article the bitch did was the one on me and my rescue puppy." Over the years Dominic and Janet had crossed swords numerous times, and Dominic had learned the hard way that the press had a way of coming out on top, of always getting in the last word. "Otherwise, I hate her writing. She has a nasty habit of always putting a negative spin on the news. She'd even make Winnie the Pooh look like Dracula if he was a public figure."

Mitchell laughed, despite himself, for once totally agreeing with the Bomb. He had no love lost for the reporter and the written barbs she had poked him with over the years. And now that her name kept coming up on this project, her probing really concerned him. "This shopping center is important, a real benefit to the Town. We can't let it get turned down," he interjected, suddenly becoming even more concerned that Janet Johnson might be getting ready to do a hatchet job on the project. Mitchell had already spent considerable time analyzing the proposal from the economic and political viewpoints. He knew from the hearings that the nearby residents were strongly against the project, but, as a seasoned politician, he knew he couldn't make everybody happy. "If Janet starts writing negative articles on the project, we're fucked. Christ, that's all we need. You know, support of the project by the Inquirer would be a real plus, perhaps we can get a favorable editorial," Mitchell suggested.

"That would be great, but the editors follow carefully what their reporter on the beat finds and writes about. So far, she hasn't come out against it-yet." Sal responded. Turning to his cousin, he said. "Let's increase our letter writing campaign, create a real letter blitz."

"Good idea, Sal. In the meantime, let's be extremely careful in our dealings with Janet. She's starting to ask a lot of questions like why hasn't the land been developed before this, and . . ."

"There's always been a lot of interest in the land," Mitchell interrupted, "but the estate's seller always wanted too much money. The children who inherited the land put it into an estate when their mother died. They all live out of state, and their image of what the land is like is unrealistic. The taxes on the land are so low there has been no incentive to develop it. They couldn't give a rat's ass about the impact on Covingford, all they want is the money."

"That's basically what I told her a few weeks ago when she called," Sal responded. "But you know her, one question leads to another."

"Another broad that just can't be satisfied," Peter joked.

"If this project goes down because of her, I am calling her editor," Mitchell responded in an angry tone.

"Don't worry about her now Keith," Sal cautioned. "You focus on the Town Manager. Sometimes he can be too independent, and too many people value his opinion."

"The crazy neighborhood, the bitchy attorney, the unsatisfied reporter, and the Town Manager on his white horse- what a combination! We've got to get a little more organized and push some more buttons. Let's get rolling some more on those letters to the editor," Peter emphasized.

Dominic suddenly stopped eating. He put down his wine. "You know Peter, I agree. The Manager is too fuckin independent. I can't get nothin on him. Kurt should have been a priest! And just because a few people came out at the hearings and opposed the project, the Commission might get wimpy, no backbone. You always get opposition, it's the Nimby's. This project is good, it's great. It's gotta go through!"

"What the fuck is NIMBY?" asked Sal.

"Not in my backyard," Dom grunted with a disgusted tone."

"OK Dom, screw em. But the hearings were very important, and they didn't go well for us. It was more than a few people opposing the project. Attorney Cimione dropped the ball; he lost control!" Sal said disgustedly. "So much for him being local and knowing everyone, especially all of the Commissioners."

"We will have to see, but he certainly was a disappointment, especially that last night of the hearing, maybe he was not the right choice after all," Peter added. "That neighborhood group surely was organized. They'll be calling the Councilors, the press, writing more letters to the editor. They already started a blog. We've got to counteract them more. We need to bring some real pressure."

"I'll work with the Councilors, and let me take care of the Town Manager," Mitchell said menacingly as he glared at Dom. "I already spoke to him on his fiscal report for the Council, and I will call him again. Leave him to me. He has to report to the Town Council and if he doesn't play ball, as a Councilor, I know how to make his life miserable, really miserable."

"Don't take too long Keith. A lot of people listen to Kurt. We don't want him influencing too many people, Town Manager or not," Sal said in a sinister voice as he glanced around the restaurant. "We don't have much time. Although the PZC has 65 days to make a decision, I think they will act sooner. They already scheduled the first special meeting just on the proposal for the 18th, less than two weeks away."

"Could be a long night. And based on how they operated in the past, they'll probably schedule another meeting right after that to actually vote, so you're right, time is flying. As far as the Town Manger goes, I'll keep a close eye on him. I'll bury him if he comes out against it," Mitchell retorted in a sinister tone. "I am getting tired of him. Maybe it's time to get rid of him." He poured Peter and himself another glass of wine and continued. "Sometimes the Manager and I cross swords. I have to sometimes remind him that he works for me and the rest of the Council, and he had better fall into line."

"That's good. He can be such a pain in the ass," Peter replied, sipping the deep red Chianti. "Umm, this wine has a nice full body to it." He reached for one of the garlic balls to go with it, but the basket was empty. Disgusted, he glanced at Dominic, who was already frantically waving for the waiter to replenish the basket yet again.

Watching Dominic resume licking the garlic off of his fingers, Mitchell continued, "I'm confident we can push this project through. As I said, I'll talk again to the other Councilors, at least my party members. Christ sake, we control the Council, we have the majority seats. We can all make a few calls to the Commissioners. Perhaps a little reminder that we appointed them. . . just like we do the Manager," he added. "Peter, have you talked to the Mayor since the hearings? After all, you were his campaign manager."

"I spoke with him over the weekend. He's coming to my office to once review the site plans."

"Good move," responded Keith. "I'll also talk with him, same political party and all that bonding stuff," he wryly snickered.

Peter, Sal and Dominic silently stared at him.

Mitchell sat back in his chair, lost for the moment in thought. *What would be the best way to bring pressure on the Town Manager? Embarrass him at a public Council meeting in front of everyone? Issue a press release on his performance not living up to expectations? Poor communications? No. Maybe an executive session on personnel, and he being the personnel. Yes, that's what I'll do. I already warned him over the phone.* Mitchell smiled as he decided on his plan of action having considered different alternatives. This was his approach to problems. Approaching his fortieth birthday, he worked in private industry as an IT specialist. He had risen through the ranks at his company through long hours, hard work, attention to detail, solving problems, and a driving desire to achieve. Within his sphere of influence, he was very effective for he carefully studied the issues and analyzed different alternatives, and could anticipate opposite opinions. Although his conclusions were not always correct, he used his speaking ability to convince others. He had perfected his style of networking, making necessary contacts with people at different levels to elicit their support for his particular project. He carried this technique over to his political world- his world where he loved to maneuver and control, a feat which he did with considerable success.

Knowledge is power Mitchell reiterated to himself. Over the years he worked on this premise. Before each Council meeting he did his homework. He read all of the information that was sent out, made phone calls to obtain input, and followed up on issues. He considered himself the point man on the Council, or at least on the majority side of the Council. The opposing side often viewed him with disdain, considering him brash, shallow, and controlling, especially Councilor Corey who wouldn't give him an inch. Even the Mayor was sometimes skeptical of his antics. "Spends too much time in front of his computer at work. He must practice talking to it," the Mayor once remarked.

"Excuse me gentlemen," the waiter suddenly interrupted Mitchell's thoughts. The waiter had quietly approached the table with a double order of the garlic balls, having admonished himself for not bringing a double order to the table when he first saw Dominic come in. *Too bad the garlic balls are complimentary and don't run up the bill and my tip!* he thought. He placed the basket on the white tablecloth and quickly retreated.

"We will need to reach out again to the Chamber of Commerce and the Economic Development Commission. They can send letters to the editor and make more calls. Their support is even more critical now since the opposition sprung up at the hearings," Mitchell commented.

"We have their backing, now we need them to do some more work," Peter said. "The Council, and the Commissioners, listen to these groups."

"And of course," Sal wryly added, "we have a few 'interested citizens' sending in letters to the editor."

"As I said, I'll keep the Manager on a short leash on this issue," Mitchell continued. "This is a key proposal, and I don't want him screwing it up with some argument over a wimpy neighborhood impact or some stupid reason like that." His tone left no question as to what he thought of Kurt.

Mitchell sat back again, his mind racing. If he played his cards right, he could get the project approved. It should be popular, except maybe for opposition from the pesky nearby neighbors. He might then even get a shot at being Mayor. And, if he really played all of his cards right, he could get rid of the Manager at the same time or at least give him enough grief to force him to resign. With him out of the picture, his own influence on the Council would be even greater. A new Town Manager would need at least a year just to come up to speed. Plus his brother would do well with the money he already invested in Pilgrim Enterprises after Mitchell had tipped him off. *Couldn't invest myself, that would be a conflict of interest* he thought with a satisfied smile. *Yes, this shopping mall could be the opportunity he had been waiting for. A triple play, the Mayor's seat, a new Town Manager, and a return on my brother's investment.* He relaxed a little. *Time for more pressure. Yes, I'll wait for a slip by the Manager, and then call for an executive session on personnel. That always starts tongues wagging.* Suddenly the grunts and slurps coming from Dominic did not bother him as much. His mind was elsewhere, already planning his strategies.

"I can make more calls to a few people too," blurted Dominic. "I seem to remember a few incidents some people may not want to be reminded of, especially one certain commissioner who had a little drinking and driving problem."

Sal glanced quickly at Peter. "Be careful with that, Dominic, and for Christ sake, don't piss off our reporter any more. She would love to nail you."

"Get off my back Sal, I know how to handle myself."

"Yeah, Dominic the 'puppy saver' – probably the only good press you got your whole life," Sal joked.

Peter said nothing. He and Sal and even Mitchell all knew Dominic's strengths, weaknesses, and his stubbornness, but especially his incredible memory for every dirty detail. Dominic never missed a trick. Mitchell shuddered slightly as he wondered if Dominic had any dirt on him.

"Pardon me gentlemen, may I take your order?" the waiter asked. He had approached their table, but they had not noticed due to the intensity of their conversation.

"Two orders of ziti and meatballs, and Dominic, are you going to have your usual double order of cheese lasagna?" Sal asked, already knowing the answer.

"Sure," replied Dominic, "with extra cheese on top." The waiter dutifully wrote down the order, one eye glancing down at Dominic. Prudently, he kept his thoughts to himself, mentally calculating the calorie and fat content of just a single order of their homemade lasagna.

"Chicken François for me," Mitchell said. The waiter took the order and left the table as quietly as he had come.

"It's agreed then, we will all start making our calls," Sal said. "And Dominic, again, watch yourself with that reporter. She is slick, and she might just sucker you into saying something."

"Screw you, Sal, I can take care of myself."

"Ok, Dominic, Ok. Let's all just be careful about who we talk to and what we say. We don't want any investigation starting on this."

"Investigation?" Mitchell asked, his eyebrows rose. "Investigation for what?"

"Nothing, Keith, nothing at all." Sal said, flickering a glance at Peter. "Just an expression whenever there is a hot issue involving the Town and the press is not in favor of what is going on. That's all."

"Oh, ok. You had me worried there for a second," replied Mitchell, but suddenly he had a fleeting feeling that everything was not ok. The relaxing glow from the strong Italian wine suddenly disappeared. His thought of becoming Mayor passed to the back of his mind. *Is there something here even I don't know about?*

TUESDAY, MARCH 5
PZC TO CONVENE NEXT WEEK
NO DISCUSSION EXPECTED ON THE
SHOPPING CENTER
By Janet Johnson
Inquirer Staff Reporter

———

COVINGFORD – Next Monday, March 11th, the Covingford Planning and Zoning Commission will meet for the first time since the contentious public hearing last week on the proposed shopping center. Chairman Bradley has said that "Since the public hearings are over, no further public input can be taken on the shopping center. It is now up to the PZC to discuss and debate the proposal, and then vote. We have to make a decision within 65 days of the close of the hearings." He also stated that the Commission planned to catch up on the backlog of other pending applications before the Commission and "there would be no discussion on the 11th on the shopping center."

Last week the Commission held three public hearings on the proposal by Pilgrim Enterprises to develop a shopping center with the grocery chain store Hoity-Toity as its anchor store and several smaller stores on a vacant 25 acre parcel of land. An angry overflow crowd of more than 250 people protested the proposal, and the final night of the hearings was quite rowdy.

A neighborhood group called SWAT is fighting the proposal, and they have hired Attorney Patricia Burns to oppose the project. "Vote No—Save Covingford" signs have been popping up on front lawns throughout town, along with a lot of signs in favor of the proposal.

Chairman Bradley has stated that the Commission will hold a special meeting on Monday, March 18, at 7:30 pm to focus exclusively on the proposal. "Nothing else will be on the Commission's agenda that night," he announced. "The meeting will be open to the public, but the public will not be allowed to speak."

Chapter 11
DOM THE BOMB

Tuesday March 5

Dominic sat in his small home office reviewing the afternoon's luncheon at the Tuscany Spa; his rescue dog Snowball lay quietly at his side. Outside, March was living up to its reputation of coming in like a lion as a blustery cold wind whipped through the State. But inside, it was warm and cozy, just the two of them. The recent Inquirer news article of him and the rescue puppy was framed and hung on his small office wall. He smiled as he read it for the 100th time, word for word. Pain in the ass that the reporter Janet was, *she finally did a good piece of work.*

January 21
ABANDONED PUPPY SAVED
BY LOCAL POLITICIAN
By Janet Johnson
Inquirer Staff Reporter

COVINGFORD – A three month old mongrel puppy scheduled to be put to sleep was saved at the last minute by local politician Dominic Columbo. The puppy, a Shih Tzu/Beagle mix, was found near death by Animal Control Officer Dog Warden Betsy Schaeffer in an old drainage ditch. "He must have gotten caught in the freezing weather we had in mid-January. He was almost frozen, shivering uncontrollably, and very thin. He was not in good condition," said Ms. Schaeffer. Despite efforts to find a loving home, there were no takers. However, according to Ms. Schaeffer, Dominic Columbo "happened to hear" that the puppy was scheduled to be euthanized and came to its rescue. "He has adopted the puppy and taken it home, and we are very appreciative of his stepping forward."

Control Officer Schaeffer said that despite several ads in the paper, no one came to claim the dog, and due to overcrowding conditions at the dog pound, it was scheduled to be put to sleep. "Dominic stepped in at the last moment and saved him. Twenty four hours later it would have been too late. And the puppy is so adorable, I just don't understand it. Must be that people were so busy they did not see the public notice on euthanizing the dog. Dom was the only one to step up. He's a real puppy hero!"

Dominic declined to identify his sources where he heard that the dog would be destroyed, but just said that it was important to him to save "this lost little creature. He is so adorable, so helpless. I just knew it was the right thing to do. He already has found a cozy corner in our house. He is right at home." Dominic said they are going to name him "Snowball" in light of the snowstorm that Dominic drove through to get to the pound in time to save him.

Dominic, chairman of the local town political committee, said "the puppy likes his red and blue blanket, a sure sign the puppy is not political."

"Yes, such a good article, she should do more of this kind of important reporting," he said out loud. Snowball looked up at him as if in total agreement, then he put his head down for some further rest, content he was keeping his savior company.

Dominic was the chairman of the local town committee, a political position he held for over eight years. The Bomb enjoyed the relative obscurity of being directly out of the public's view. He was not elected, yet at the same time, he exercised considerable influence on public policy decisions. No pay, but it did give him power. Although no written job description or formal organizational chart existed for the party chairman, Dominic survived by his ability to sway key votes in the "right direction" when the situation and time required it. This ability, plus his close connections to the Garganos, helped him maintain his power broker position despite an almost universal strong dislike of his slovenly appearance and behavior. He relished in his perceived power.

On a daily basis he made deals and agreements. Networking and making deals were his stock and trade. The fact that many of these deals would not have passed the scrutiny of the limelight focus on them did not bother him. Rarely was he in the public's view; he left that to the elected public officials. His world was behind the scenes - a murky world of closed-door meetings and secret deals that affected public policy.

The Bomb absorbed information on people like a blotter. He was not afraid to use this information when the occasion called for it. This was his world, and he was good at it. He had contacts all over the place. He knew a little about everyone, especially if it contained a little dirt. He kept track of tid-bits of overheard information; the fact that it was only rumor did not matter, truth was often immaterial. The juicer the information, the better. The fact that someone else had even mentioned an incident was sufficient basis for remembering the item. After all, he rationalized, *if two people discussed the issue, something had to be there.* Dominic never knew when the information might come in handy. At the right time it could provide him with that little extra leverage.

Dominic made sure he attended all of the political functions. He realized it was also important to maintain his contacts especially with Peter and Sal. In their youth, they had all grown up in the same neighborhood in the Frog Hollow section of Hartford. The childhood friendship continued over the years, despite the development of Dom's obnoxious habits. Sal and Pete had gotten so accustomed to Dom that they just accepted his quirks in stride. Dom's connection to these powerful individuals was most helpful. He understood the importance of this relationship, and he made sure that it was well known to others. On more than one occasion he had made passing references to being with the Garganos on a regular basis. He felt no shame in dropping their names especially in town business, where they were quite influential. He was keenly aware of the issues before the Town, and closely followed the Town Council, Board of Education, and most importantly, the Zoning Commission. He made especially sure he involved himself in the middle of all the major proposals especially the Zoning Commission since they were the board that controlled the local land use decisions.

Although he possessed a knack for numbers, Dominic dropped out of college after his freshman year. He started taking night courses at the local community college in bookkeeping and accounting. Despite his ability to perform well in the class, he lacked the fortitude and perseverance to become an accountant or a CPA. He did discover however, that he had a gift to remember minute trivia about people, *especially* if it involved dirt. He pictured himself as a street fighter, at least with words. The 16th century Italian political theorist Machiavelli was his hero, and he kept a copy of Machiavelli's "The Prince" on his desk. As chairman of the town committee, he could use all of the deviant strategies he could conjure up, and then some. He was very effective. He envisioned himself as a big roller, after all he was "Dom the Bomb," an important man. This role offered an outlet and provided a sharp contrast to his mundane daytime job as a bookkeeper in a local hardware store.

Dominic drove a large ten year old long black Lincoln, purchased used from a car rental agency. Although he told people this large car was needed for his large size, he firmly believed it added to his stature and importance. His wife, Barbara, a blond by bottle, sported an aging red MG Roadster. Her car, also past its prime, was well known to the local mechanics. Only recently she had problems with the local mechanics when they told her it would take a few days to repair the car because of the difficulty in getting parts. She had vehemently argued that "It had to be ready by tomorrow, or my husband. . ." emphasizing the words "my husband," pausing just long enough to let those words sink in, "or my husband will be very upset, very upset."

"Sorry ma'am, best we can do is 48 hours. We have to order the parts for these foreign cars, not stock items. And. . ." Bobby, the chief mechanic continued in a straight somber expression, "you have to pay in advance for the parts – standard policy." Bobby's young assistant suddenly dropped his wrench and left the room, doubled over in a stifled laugh.

"My husband will not be happy," she persisted, oblivious to the coincidence of the noisy compressor going on each time she started to speak. "I'm a busy person and I need my car. Do you know, do you really know who my husband is?" she screamed over the banging compressor. The compressor suddenly stopped, and her shrill voice filled the silence of the garage. Even she was startled at the loudness of her own voice. She stood there, her mouth open, red faced and suddenly embarrassed.

"Yes ma'am," Bobby replied quietly, "that'll be $475. . . in advance."

Barbara's convoluted image of her husband's reputation was bigger than the value of her aging MG. Both considered themselves very important people. They liked the images of their prestigious Lincoln and the classic MG. The fact that the cars were several years old was not an issue, just a factor of the "bad luck" they had experienced in recent years at the casinos. Several times a year they would drive down to Atlantic City in New Jersey to tempt the gambling gods, trips which recently had not gone in their favor. They chose not to gamble at the two Indian casinos in their own backyard in eastern Connecticut, preferring the more distant location away from their home where they would not be recognized.

Despite this out of state location, a brief article in last year's Hartford Inquirer by reporter Janet Johnson had revealed that Dominic and Barbara had run up a gambling debt of over $100,000 at a certain casino in New Jersey. Dominic was furious over the article and threatened a lawsuit. On the advice of her editor, Janet did not do a follow up story although she had obtained considerably more information. Her editor also advised her she might want to consider a soft story on Dominic in the future, something not as threatening. In a weak moment, Janet capitulated and wrote an article on the abandoned puppy that Dominic had saved.

Janet did learn that Dominic's in-laws had helped bail them out at the time, but that no more money would be forthcoming. His wife's parents claimed that now they were both retired, they just couldn't help pay anymore. There were persistent whispers in Covingford that Dominic and Barbara were still visiting the casinos and their luck recently had gone from bad to worse. Janet's sources advised her that things had gotten more serious for Dom and Barbara, very serious. Janet continued to keep good notes and made more discreet inquiries, and kept her powder dry.

Dominic had developed a skill of talking with people and then suddenly inserting questions into the conversation. The questions seemed innocent enough, and often appeared not relevant to the conversation - at least not to the person with whom he was talking. This style frequently caught people off guard, and the little bits of information that people innocently gave up often came back to haunt them years later. Without realizing it, they would automatically respond to his questions, and suddenly, they were left with an uneasy feeling about the information they has just innocently conveyed to him. People were never sure why they had that feeling, although some did find out years later when a related incident, however trivial, was suddenly brought up, often at a most inopportune moment.

Dominic was well aware of how he manipulated conversations. He knew he had the uncanny ability to remember the minutest detail about a person for years. It was always fun to put a little different spin on the details to spice them up, especially when it caused some additional discomfort to the person who was the object of his barbs. He especially enjoyed the annual summer political picnic, a hotbed of rumors. And last summer had been especially fruitful.

Dominic shifted his massive weight in his worn leather chair, as he carefully reviewed the afternoon's earlier luncheon conversation with Peter, Sal, and Keith; he absent mindedly scratched Snowball's ear. His recent encounter with Louie "The Enforcer" after the shopping center hearings weighed heavily on him. He had made some calls the morning after his encounter with the "Enforcer," but now things were moving even faster. "Damn," he murmured aloud, causing Snowball to look up at him and cock his head, "even Peter and Sal are concerned, and Keith didn't seem too happy." He looked at Snowball and spoke directly to him. "That Mitchell is such a political prick, always out for number one. *I'll let him handle the Town Manager for now, much as I would love to nail that bastard. Two bastards together,*" he grinned. Snowball stared at him, head tilted, taking in every word. "It really is time to put some real pressure on some people. Yes, time to take the gloves off and contact my favorite Zoning Commissioner, Mr. Katz, and" glancing down at Snowball, he continued "casually remind him of his little indiscretion last winter. He certainly didn't appreciate my bringing it up to him last summer at the picnic. Yes, it's time to play hardball."

Dominic knew that this deal would be the most important one of his life; it would wipe away his heavy debt. Looking down at Snowball he exclaimed, "I will be a free man, at the top of the hill again." Snowball stared at the Bomb, nodded, and then lowered his head and stretched out on the floor at this master's feet, his listening duty done. Time for his early afternoon siesta, after all, he needed to be ready for his late afternoon snooze.

March 6th
Letters to the Editor
The Inquirer

Need Tax Revenue-Vote YES

Pilgrim Enterprises is proposing a project that will be a major benefit to our community for years to come. Increased tax revenue, more jobs, cleaning up of an overgrown weed filled area, and an upscale food market to boot. All positive benefits to Covingford. What is there not to like? Our taxes are going through the roof, our high school has to be totally renovated, where does it stop? Come on Commissioners, vote YES.

Victor Bernstein
Covingford

Chapter 12
THE SUMMER PICNIC

Tuesday March 5

As Snowball stretched out for his early afternoon rest, Dominic's thoughts drifted back to the previous summer's political picnic. The oppressive heat had totally blanketed the east coast as the weather front sat immobilized over New England. The gathering was the political event of the year, a time for town politicians to get together, enjoy good food, cold drinks, and talk politics, politics, and more politics. Dominic relished the annual event, almost a carnival atmosphere at one of the local parks. He could guzzle down hot dogs loaded with mustard, relish, and sauerkraut, all washed down with cold keg beer. The past summer's event had been especially fruitful, aided by the oppressive heat with the resulting extra cold beer that flowed, a proven recipe to loosen the tongue. He had been lucky and picked up pieces of gossip and some sordid stories. Stories he would remember when the appropriate time came, a time when he could use some of his knowledge to cause someone a little embarrassment. *Yes, it had been a good day, and now, yes now, was the time to put to put the fruits of his labor to work.*

Dominic recalled that he had spotted Jerry Katz, the newest member of the Zoning Commission. Jerry was having a good time, enjoying the day, the food and the crowd of people. Dominic had sauntered over, puffing on his cigar and ignoring the happy adults and playing children he passed. His eyes had focused on his unwary prey.

"Hi Jerry."

Jerry turned at the sound of his name, his facial expression immediately dropped when he saw Dominic. "Hello Dominic," was the best he could muster. He had not noticed Dominic coming up to him, despite Dominic's bright red Bermuda shorts, yellow palm tree shirt, smelly cigar, and size twelve running shoes that had never seen movement faster than a waddle.

"Boy, that hot dog looks good smothered in all that mustard and sauerkraut." Dominic replied.

"Emm" Jerry acknowledged, trying to reply between bites as he worked feverishly to avoid dropping the sauerkraut all over his brightly flowered shirt. He tried to focus on that task, half acknowledging Dominic's uninvited presence.

"Yeah," Dominic continued, "nothing like an ice cold beer and a dog cooked outside over the grill." Dominic did not miss the body language of Jerry, which was screaming 'get out of my face.' "I had a couple of dogs myself. The beer was great washing it down." The sweat on Dominic's wrinkled face was testimony to the 90-degree temperature and high humidity at the outing. Even his eyebrows were dripping.

"You said it Dom," Jerry replied and thought to himself, *probably a half a dozen dogs is more like it you fat slob.* A piece of the smothered dog wiggled down Jerry's throat. "This is my second dog and third beer," he continued as he licked the brown mustard off his fingers. "Food always tastes better at these outings. And look at all of the activity going on here," he half pointed out with his head and his half eaten hot dog. He purposely avoided eye contact with the fat man in front of him, hoping he would go away.

"You're right Jerry, just look at those kids swimming, really enjoying themselves. Softball, Frisbee, games all over the place, it's quite a crowd. Even the dogs get to play. What a great life for them. I love dogs. Good times for everybody."

"Good for you, get a puppy!" Jerry said sarcastically.

"Maybe I will," Dominic retorted. "Got to watch out for God's little creatures you know. So here we are, perfect weather, although a bit warm. What could be better?" Dominic continued as he wiped the beads of perspiration from his brow with his wrinkled and well-used handkerchief. "But this hot weather makes those cold beers taste all the better, don't ya think?"

"Yup. Couldn't ask for a better day, everything is perfect," Jerry replied as he took another sip of beer, trying his best not to prolong the conversation. The effects of the beers made him more relaxed than he normally would have been in a conversation with Dominic.

"I agree. It's a perfect day. But Jerry, just don't have too many beers, *especially* if you are going to drive," Dominic continued in a nonchalant tone.

Jerry stared at Dominic, not saying a word. His hand froze as he held the dripping hot dog inches from his mouth.

"As I said Jerry, it ain't good to drink and drive – never can tell what can happen."

"Sure Dom."

"But you have experience with drinking and driving, don't you Jerry?" Dominic said in a lowered sinister tone; he could feel himself warming up. He was coming into his stride.

Wh . . . What. . . did you say?"

"Just making an observation about driving and drinking, never know what could be the result," Dominic continued as he half looked away at many activities going on. One man was tossing a Frisbee to his dog, which jumped up trying to snatch the disk in his teeth. A small crowd of children cheered when the dog jumped. Without directly looking at Jerry, he observed the impact his words were having.

Jerry's head was suddenly throbbing with anxiety. He stopped eating his hot dog and moved it away from this mouth. "What the hell are you talking about? I'm always a careful driver," he retorted, angry with himself for sounding so defensive.

"Are you? Well, no problem. We just don't want to have another incident like we had this past winter, do we?" Dominic concluded with a smirk, his half closed beady eyes looking directly at Jerry. Sweat poured off of his forehead.

"What. . . What the hell are you talking about?" Jerry responded with a sickening feeling in his stomach. The recoil of his head could not have been sharper if the hot dog had bitten him. Jerry's appetite suddenly disappeared, the idyllic mood of the day disappeared. The busy crowd around him suddenly did not exist. The cheers from the children were blotted out. He quickly glanced around to see if anyone was within earshot. His thoughts raced back to the incident, an indiscretion on the previous winter's night.

"Remember?" Dominic's tone snapped Jerry's brief lapse. "Oh, I was just thinking back to that incident last December involving drinking and driving. Funny how sometimes drunk driving doesn't make the newspapers," Dominic had said in his best casual tone, his smirk reflected his enjoyment at suddenly having made Jerry immensely uncomfortable. "If my memory serves me correctly, you were just appointed a member of the Zoning Commission. You're now a BMOC, no?"

"Big Man on Campus!! No way, screw you. What's the point of this Dominic?" His voice held a tone of confidence he did not feel.

"The point is. . ." Dominic hesitated, enjoying the impact he knew his next few words would have. "The point is, I guess it pays to have friends in the right place at the right time, doesn't it Jerry?"

Jerry started to blurt out something but caught himself. He collected his thoughts. *Damn those beers.* "That was seven months ago. Nothing ever came of it. No big deal." *You bastard.*

"Well, as I recall it Jerry, you were stopped by the cops. Something about, ahh, drunken driving. Alcohol blood level of 1.7, well above our beloved State's legal limit of 0.8. Funny how there was no formal report. That incident just kinda dropped with a minimum of fanfare, poof, gone." Dominic made an ok with his fat fingers, and then threw his hand up in the air, opening it as it went.

Jerry stood there dumbfounded. "How the hell do you know about that incident?" he managed to get out, his throat suddenly dry.

"Well Jerry, let's just say it's a good thing our ace reporter Janet Johnson didn't hear about it. Can you imagine the headlines? 'Newly appointed Zoning Commissioner Katz stopped for drunken driving-no ticket issued.' "

Jerry's body trembled with a sudden chill despite the high temperature and oppressive humidity. A light breeze had picked up. The noise of the picnic seemed to disappear. "That. . . That incident involved a visit to my wife who was in the hospital for major surgery. She was having a cancerous tumor removed and the Doctors were concerned, very concerned. " Jerry blurted out, despite himself. "I had stopped with some close friends for a few drinks to talk about the impact the malignancy suddenly had on my life and my wife; we're married for twenty seven years, ya know. I needed that unwinding, it was a tough time for me."

"Touching."

Jerry was so wrapped up in reliving the incident he missed Dominic's sarcasm. "As you know, Dom, she died shortly thereafter." He hesitated, lost in the painful memory, then continued. "On my drive home that night I was stopped by a local officer who claimed I went through a red light, no big deal."

"I understood that officer had followed your weaving car down the block before he stopped you," Dominic continued. He noticed the dog had caught the Frisbee, but was not returning it to his master. The children were all running around the dog, yelling and laughing.

"There was no ticket issued. The officer was very understanding, he knew my wife."

"Sure was. As I heard it, he then even drove you home, courtesy of our local taxpayers."

"Screw you Dominic. It's none of your goddamn business," Jerry's defensiveness suddenly turned to anger. Throwing his half eaten hot dog on the ground, he turned away from Dominic in a feeble attempt to snub him. "Don't worry Jerry," Dominic continued undaunted, his wry grin covering his fat face, his eyes almost lost in layers of flesh. He glanced downward at his ever-present cigar, and flicked the ashes off it. "I'm not inclined to reveal anything about it. These things happen, you know. Some people are just lucky that they never make the newspaper, don't you think?"

Jerry stormed away without looking back. He almost knocked over a couple standing near the crowd which was absorbed by the dog as it continued to amuse the gaggle of laughing children. He was suddenly oblivious to the happy times people were having as he pushed through the crowd, intent only on getting away from "the Bomb."

The incident had made Dominic's day he recalled with a satisfied smirk as he sat in his home office gazing out at the snow. "It does pay to have people in vulnerable positions, never can tell when one might need a little favor," he said aloud to Snowball. "And the Zoning Commission is as good as any. Plus, it sure doesn't hurt to have contacts, especially in the police department. Yes, that little incident last summer is sure going to come in handy right now, very handy," Dominic mused as he reached down and petted the head of Snowball, his one faithful friend. Snowball gazed up at him, simple love for his master, his head cocked in full understanding. Dominic continued in the one-way conversation. "I'm sure Jerry will not want that story coming out, especially now since he is such an important member of the Zoning Commission that has to make such an important decision. Peter and Sal are gonna love this maneuver, can't wait to call Jerry." He took a deep drag on his cigar, blew a few circles, and puffed away contently. He was, after all, Dom the Bomb. Snowball nodded his head in total concurrence.

Chapter 13
TOWN MANAGER'S LUNCH & PUBLIC WORKS

Wednesday, March 6

"Liz, I'm going out for lunch," Kurt said as he slipped on his heavy winter parka and rubber boots and quietly stepped out of the Town Manager's office. He took the stairwell down to the main floor and carefully made his way down the front steps and onto the sidewalk, still partially covered with ice. *Hmmm, needs more sand, I'd better call public works.* His thoughts shifted to the anticipated taste of a hot corned beef sandwich on toasted rye, plenty of spicy mustard, and a good kosher dill pickle down at Chuck's. "The best deli around," he had often commented.

Mr. Town Manager, I need to talk to you," an elderly man in his late seventies suddenly appeared as Kurt turned the corner right in front of Chuck's deli. He shook his finger in Kurt's face, clearly agitated about something. Wearing a long gray winter coat with a heavy woolen cap pulled down over his ears, his breath in the cold air formed a vapor cloud between Kurt and himself. Taking advantage of the unexpected encounter with the Manager, he immediately proceeded without introducing himself.

"Our senior van is taking too long to pick us up and carry us to the senior center. I spent over 45 minutes this morning on the van - that's way too long. Can't you shorten up the route or change how pickups are made?" Without waiting for a reply he continued on. "I'm not the only one who feels this way. There's a group of us at the Senior Center who have been talking about this. We're gonna get a petition together and send it to the Town Council. We're also gonna call the TV station and the newspaper. It ain't right."

"Did you talk to the Senior Center Director?"

"Ahh, she won't do anything." The man rubbed his hands together to warm them, sidestepping the question posed to him.

"Start there anyway. I'll also talk to her. I do know that there are more seniors then ever using the vans - must be the good cooking at the Center, don't you think?" Kurt joked. The man, so focused on his problem, missed the humor. "I'll go over the schedule with the Center Director and see if anything can be done," Kurt continued.

"I appreciate it, but as I said, we're not happy. I'll try and convince the others to wait on the petition and the press - give you some time to look into it."

"Thanks. I'll call this afternoon," Kurt offered. The senior, satisfied that he had made his point with the Manager, continued on his way, stepping carefully along the icy sidewalk. He was anxious to get back to the Center and tell the rest of his companions he had talked "personally" with the Town Manager and given him a piece of his mind. And yes, because of his complaint he could tell the group that "the Manager is going to look immediately into our problem. He was now fully informed of this pressing problem that we seniors are facing."

"Hi Kurt, how's things?" Chuck Cohen, the deli owner yelled over to Kurt as he entered the door, seeing the dialogue he had just been trapped in. "Come on in and grab a seat. We've some nice specials today-roast beef, hot pastrami, pasta with peppers."

"How's the corned beef today?" Kurt responded, thankful for the brief change away from town business.

"Great, want it on a hard roll or on rye with our special mustard?"

"The rye with mustard is fine, grilled, and throw in one of your pickles from the vat, and a cold cola."

"You got it," Chuck responded cheerfully. "Quite an unusual storm last night. I got up this morning at 4 am to get today's food ready and I couldn't believe my eyes. Snow and ice all over. When I went to bed around 9, nothing was happening. Forecast said something about snow flurries."

"It started around 11, just as I was going to bed."

"Snow flurries! So much for Doppler radar and all the fancy stuff," Chuck responded with a wry grin.

Kurt laughed as he grabbed his sandwich and found a chair at a small table in the corner. He browsed through the newspaper to catch up on the local news involving both Covingford and the other nearby towns. He had observed over the years that the same issues affected all the different towns, with the only difference being in the names and personalities. It seemed each town preferred to create the wheel. *Nothing like home rule* he thought, referring to the government philosophy that each town had the right to self-governance with a minimum of interference from the state. He quietly read, enjoying the corned beef and the cold soda. He savored these quiet moments, away from the telephone and the constant conversations of the job.

"Any dessert today Kurt?" Chuck asked, interrupting his reading.

"No, that's all. Just the bill. Corn beef was great today."

"It's always great. You're just hungry today - must be your late night meetings. Did you go to any of the zoning hearings last week on the new shopping center? "

"Sure did. They were long ones."

"I wanted to go, but I have to get up too early for this deli to stay up late at those meetings. The project could be good for town, bring in some real tax money. Help with our taxes here, always going up."

"Could be. A lot of people came out against the proposal though. The last night of the hearing got pretty hot."

"Yea, I read that. That reporter Janet what's-her-name does a good job of following what's going on. Nobody wants any changes in their back yard. Town's gotta grow though." Chuck replied. "Next time you're in, try the pastrami. People really like my pastrami with melted cheese, onion, sauerkraut, and then smothered in Thousand Island dressing, all enclosed in seeded rye bread. I then grill it on my super-hot grill. Giant dill pickle on the side. Delish! 'Chuck's Special' I call it. A big mover. And wash it all down with cold Birch Beer," he added with a broad proud grin.

"You sold me. I'll try it next week, Chuck. Thanks. Gotta run over to public works." Kurt replied.

"With all this snow, I'm sure they're getting their overtime in this year." Chuck responded.

"Those guys earn it. It's no fun on these cold winter nights to plow and sand all night."

"See you next week, remember, 'Chuck's Special', pastrami with the works," he smiled proudly.

Kurt slipped out the door, bundling up his overcoat against the cold.

The Public Works Department, located about two miles from the Town Hall, was just on the outskirts of Covingford. A large manufactured building housed the offices and the garages for the public works equipment. Off to one side stood the sand and salt shed, a busy place in the winter storms. A large pay loader stood in front of the shed, its diesel motor still running despite the absence of an operator. The mixing of sand and salt for the winter storms was a continual event, day and night.

"Snow flurries my ass," exclaimed Fran Collins, Director of Public Works, as soon as he saw Kurt getting out of his municipal Ford Taurus.

Kurt grinned at the greeting, so typical of his friend Collins.

"I'm going to call the weather man and invite him to ride on our plows to see what his 'snow flurries' are really like. One of these days he may actually stick his head out the window and see what the hell is really going on," Fran continued in a huffy tone.

"I'm sure he would just love to hear from you Fran." Kurt replied. "When did you get called out last night?"

"Around 11:30 last night the police dispatcher called. It wouldn't have been so bad if we had warning, but this damn storm came outta nowhere. And here it is almost mid-March. Damn winter won't quit. Last time I'll believe that groundhog and the end of winter. I had to call the guys out of some nice warm beds. If we had known it was coming, I could've kept a few guys here on standby at the garage, and we could have gotten a jump start on it."

A congenial individual in his mid-forties, Fran had been Public Works Director for seven years. Standing 5'8" tall with sandy hair, which never seemed fully combed, he ran a tight ship. He had a manner about him that made people comfortable in talking with him. His steady gaze with his steel gray eyes made people quickly realize that beneath that easy going style was an inner strength.

Fran had started as a driver in the department twenty years earlier, his first job after a tour of duty with the Army. He had moved up in the public works responsibilities, often taking advantage of the different training opportunities that were offered. His promotion to Director by Kurt surprised no one, and he met expectations as a tough but fair boss. He demanded a lot of his crew, much to the chagrin of a few who felt they were lifers who could coast to retirement in the department. That notion was soon dispelled, as Fran often worked alongside of them to see that the job got done right. A few of the newer employees had decided it was best to leave. A native of the town, he had the pulse on many local issues and often knew things before Kurt. On more than one occasion, he had given Kurt heads up when something was about to break.

"Long Council meeting Monday night?" Fran half asked and half stated. "Sure seems to be a number of topics going on in this town. Major shopping center, drainage issues, trash contract renewals, sewer hook-ups. Lots of letters to the editor. Did any citizens come to the meeting to complain about the pile of trash in the middle of Long Hill Road?"

"No. What's the problem?" Kurt asked with a puzzled look on his face.

"No problem now. It seems our trash hauler thought he could leave trash in the middle of a private road."

"Oh? Their contract is for residential pickup. And private contractors can hire them directly for their own commercial operations. So what happened on the private road?"

"I tried to reach you yesterday to tip you off, but I couldn't get hold of you. That contractor building the new homes on Long Hill Road didn't pay the trash contractor, so the contractor went up and just took away his dumpster, a big 30 cubic yard one."

"The contractor does own the dumpster," Kurt replied, knowing there was more to come.

"Yup, he sure does, but he felt he didn't own the trash since it wasn't paid for. So, before he took it, he returned the trash to the contractor - unloaded it - right onto the street and . . ."

"He what?" Kurt stopped in his tracks and stared at Fran, who was grinning ear to ear.

"Yup. Unloaded it right in the middle of the street, all 30 cubic yards. Trash all over the place." Fran enjoyed telling the story, seeing the reaction it had on Kurt. "Problem was, or is, at least for the developer, he still owns the street, not the town."

'You're right. The Town has not yet accepted it." Kurt responded with a small whistle.

"Amazing. These trash contractors never cease to surprise me. And we are evaluating the trash bids as we speak. So what did you do Mr. Director?"

"Well, I called the trash hauler, and we had a little discussion on their maneuver. I also had the police department pay them a visit and they had a 'friendly chat' about health laws, vehicle registration, broken signal lights, and on a whole bunch of other obscure laws the cops insisted were on the books." Fran's breath mixed with the cold air, forming one large vapor cloud.

"And?

"Let's just say the matter has been resolved." Fran's broad grin convinced Kurt that the matter was well taken care of.

"I'm sure the police were very persuasive."

"I guess so. One of the officers mentioned to me that it seems that a few of their trucks may not have been current in their registration. . . or something like that. But, from what I hear, the matter was quickly taken care of and the trash picked up. Good thing, since the neighbors were really mad at both the developer and the trash contractor."

"Where does it stand right now?" Kurt asked, still shaking his head over the incredible story.

"The trash collectors are still mad that they did not get paid yet for the dumpster. I hear the developer may be filing for bankruptcy, and that housing development is only partially completed."

"That could be a problem," Kurt replied, raising his eyebrows. "We have a road bond posted by the developer to insure the road gets built if the contractor goes belly up. So if he does declare bankruptcy, we call the bond and that brings in the contractor's insurance company. The insurance bond guarantees that the road will be completed, and the insurance company then has to pay to finish the road and other public improvements. It's a real black eye for the builder, and can hurt him in the future. It's a real pain to call the bond, however, and it can get sticky. It delays the project, and raises all kinds of issues, such as insuring that all the correct labor rates were paid right along, all taxes paid, insurance coverage is maintained, just to name a few. I had to call a bond a few years ago on the new volunteer fire department building."

"I remember that. You always have fun things to deal with," Fran said with a grin, a mile wide, a cigarette dangling from his mouth. Kurt could not understand how it defied the laws of gravity as it just hung on the edge of Fran's lips.

"By the way Fran, the new town ordinance bans smoking on town property, and it will be effective in two weeks."

"More damn government regulations. Will it also apply to the town snow plows?"

"Yup."

"That's going to be a problem. Some of our guys smoke all the time during these long winter nights when they are out snow plowing all by themselves."

"I know Fran, but it's just not Covingford. All municipalities are going in this direction. Anyway, getting back to our friends the trash collectors, they are always such a pleasure to deal with, that's for sure," Kurt continued, as he watched one of the town's large snow fighters pull out of the garage, its heavy plow hanging off the front of the truck. A small pyramid of sand and salt weighing heavily on its back.

Following Kurt's gaze, Fran quickly changed topics. "Our trucks really take a beating during these winter storms. Look at that truck, the heavy plow in the front, and the sand and salt mixture overflowing in the back - that's a lot of weight, especially on the hilly roads in this town."

"That's for sure. Break any axles last night?"

"Not last night. During major winter storms we'll go through an axle or two. Once in a while we'll also drop a transmission. Then we get the broken motors on the sanders on the rear of the trucks - you name it, if it is weak, these storms will finish it off."

"Our hard winters certainly take their toll on our equipment, that's for sure."

"What happens if that shopping center gets approved?" Fran asked, suddenly changing topics. "More traffic on our roads that we have to plow and maintain? We have enough to do as it is and we can't keep up. Rumor has it that it is going to get approved, and there is some big money behind it. And get this. One of my guys was in a gin mill the other night and there was some discussion of the project getting approved, with or without the Town Manager! What the hell does that mean? Are you getting pressure on it?" Fran asked with a concerned tone.

"Let's just say it is a topic of discussion with certain council members," Kurt replied, a worried look spreading across his face.

"There are some funny things going on, but nothing I can pin down just yet. Any names mentioned?"

"Columbo's name came up, along with the Garganos. They seem to get involved in an awful lot of things outside of their businesses."

"I sometimes think town affairs are their first business and everything else comes in second," Kurt offered. "They really get involved, almost an obsession, and very emotional."

"I know what you mean. Kurt, you should be aware there were a few other names popping up of some people from outside of Covington. Didn't recognize the names, but the references involving them were not one that they would be candidates to be Boy Scout leaders. I'll keep my ears open and let you know if I hear anything else. Oh, one more thing," Fran said in a lower voice. "There's something funny about that property."

"What do you mean 'funny'?" Kurt was suddenly totally focused on what Fran just said. He pulled up the collar on his coat as the wind picked up, delivering a chilling cutting cold.

"When I was kid I used to hunt and fish in that area. Small stuff – rabbits, squirrels, mink - And then one day it seems as though everything stopped. No more wildlife, no more fish. No one could explain it. We all heard stories of an evil spell coming over the area. That's all we needed to hear at that age. We stopped going there."

"What else do you remember about it Fran? Was there an incident or something?"

"No. Nothing specific that I can remember. But I was just a kid then. There were some rumors of trucks going onto the site in the middle of the night, but that was a long long time ago. Now the property just sits vacant, collecting trash. What an eyesore. It's almost like a dead zone. Don't even hear birds when I go by the site."

"Yea, I noticed that but never paid too much attention to it. The site was always just there, nothing special to attract attention-until the last few months. If you hear of anything about the property, or any names, and I mean ANYTHING, let me know right away."

"You got it, Kurt, no problembo."

"Thanks Fran, gotta get back to the office, see you."

Liz greeted Kurt when he returned and followed him into his office as he hung up his coat. The frown on her face, along with the worried tone in her voice gave him a heads up some bad news was on its way. "Councilor Mitchell called about 45 minutes ago and said he was very anxious to talk with you. I asked him the topic and he replied in his usual curt tone, no pun intended," she added. "'Just have him call me,' was all he said, and then just hung up. Such a pleasant character. And, this gentleman in the outer office says he has to speak with you right away, but wouldn't say why."

"Thanks Liz, I'll call Mitchell in a few minutes. Any other calls?"

"No, things quieted down right after you left for lunch. Probably because the plows finished all their routes and are just doing clean-up operations. The strong sun this time of year always helps the salt to work on the roads." Liz Kelsey had not served as secretary for two different Town Managers over a fifteen year period without picking up on the conditions of winter weather operations. She also made it her business to know all the councilors, and a little about each one.

"OK Liz, thanks, please send in the gentleman."

The man entered the office and walked right up to Kurt's desk. Kurt noticed he was a short thin individual, early fifties, dark glasses, hair sticking out from under a black winter wool hat. He sported a serious look on his face as he stared down at Kurt.

"Hi, I'm Kurt Thomas, can I help you?" Kurt stood and extended his hand.

"Sure can," the man responded as he reached into his coat and instead of shaking Kurt's hand, slapped a subpoena into Kurt's extended hand. "You have to be in court Friday morning," he said in a rough tone, "10:00 sharp, on the Gainer drainage dispute that the town didn't resolve last year. I am also serving papers on your town engineer and your public works director. Please bring all of your records that you have on this issue."

Kurt scanned the subpoena. "That's the day after tomorrow," he responded with a low whistle. "It will take time to pull all of those records, and I am out of the office all day tomorrow. Usually I get a heads up call from the attorney with a good amount of lead time."

Shrugging his shoulders, the sheriff, having processed the paperwork, turned to leave. "Hey, I just deliver the message, not create it. Attorney Meyers issued it. Here's your two dollars for court travel fees. Have a nice day." He turned and abruptly left.

"Sorry Kurt, he's new and I didn't have a clue as to why he was here," Liz said in an apologetic tone as she stood in the doorway. "He wouldn't give his name or why he wanted to see you."

"It's ok. He's only doing his job, but these subpoenas are a pain in the neck. Usually I get notice that they are coming. Meyers is new in town, and hasn't learned yet the professional relationships we have with the attorneys and the courtesies we extend to each other. Long as I'm on a roll, I better call Mitchell now and see what's bugging him." He picked up the phone, apprehensive of the direction the phone call would be going.

"Hi Keith, Kurt here, Liz said you called."

"Still waiting for the financial report we talked about last week. But even more important, I want to review with you the proposed shopping center just to be sure we are all on the same page. You gave the Town Council an upbeat report on it when it was first announced, talking about the value to our tax base, local employment, etc. etc., but recently you have been fairly quiet on the proposal. No change of heart I hope," Keith growled in a menacing tone.

"I was waiting for the public hearings to get more input, see what other viewpoints there might be on the proposals. Best way to learn," Kurt said, ignoring Keith's tone. "And the hearings did bring out some negatives on the project. It certainly has its pros and cons as we all learned last week from Attorney Burns and her group. It certainly seems to be a mixed bag."

"Mixed bag, my ass!" Keith exploded. "I'm telling you this is a good project for the town. It helps our economic development and our tax base. You keep telling us each year that you need more staff, need to increase the police department, renovate the high school, etc. etc. Well this proposal will increase our tax revenues and take care of those problems. It'll even bring more employment. Who knows, you might even get that assistant you been crying about," he added sarcastically.

"No argument there. But there is a price, and that price will be more traffic and an adverse impact on that neighborhood. A lot of those people are very concerned, they were angry, and scared, at the hearings."

"I'm telling you this is good for the town," Keith almost screamed. "Don't forget that! This project has to go forward. Economic development is the stated goal of this Council, and you had better not read us wrong. Get with the program. Remember, the Manager serves at the pleasure of the Council!"

Another not so veiled threat from my favorite Council member. He certainly is beating the drum on this proposal. Wonder if there is some other reason he's so gung ho on this project. Kurt tapped his pencil lightly on his blotter. "I'm gonna finish up the analysis and get it out to the Council next week. Remember Keith, it's the Zoning Commission that has to make the decision, not the Council," Kurt finished off with a slight rebuff.

"I'm sure they'll make the right decision. You just take care of what information you put out, and watch what you say. I'll wait for that report, next week!" The line went dead.

Always a happy camper, thought Kurt. *He really is wound up on this one. Wonder why, what's he up to this time?*

Letters to the Editor
The Inquirer

A Wonderful Opportunity
My dear friend Katherine was at the PZC meeting last week and told me all about the excitement over the planned new shopping center. We spend a lot of time talking about it when we get together to sit and knit in my living room. Katherine is a dear sweet friend and she loved what that lady lawyer had to say. But I think Kay was wrong when she said we should fear this wonderful plan that would bring all those nice new stores right across from my house.

As a senior citizen I don't get out much anymore and depend on the Senior Center van or friends to take me shopping and to the drugstore way downtown on Main Street. (My kids and grandchildren all live out of state.) It'd be so exciting to have some stores right across the street from my house. I can't wait to sit on my porch and look down the hill to see all the cars and the happy families going to and from the center. What a joy it'll be to see more kids happily going shopping with their mommies and daddies.

I love my house and my neighbors, but sometimes it gets so quiet here—it actually gets lonely. Maybe with some new stores right across the street I could get out more since I could safely cross the street as I push my walker across at the crosswalk. (There WILL be a crosswalk and traffic light, won't there? I sure hope so!)

Finally maybe having some new stores and lots of new jobs nearby might even help the value of my house. Wouldn't that be wonderful? Especially since I live on just my Social Security and a very small pension which don't go very far anymore. The new taxes the stores will bring into town would be a true blessing, believe me.

I hear the stores area will be surrounded by lovely trees and colorful flowers. What a joy! It will be such fun to look down at this beautiful garden area instead of the trash filled woods like it is now. Anyhow I just wanted to tell you that I think this new plan is a GREAT idea and I hope the town fathers approve it when they vote. Thank you very much for listening. You are <u>such</u> a sweet boy and do such a good job at the paper—your mother must be very proud of you indeed.

Sincerely,
Thelma Augustana Clark
Lifelong resident of Covingford

Chapter 14
THE BOMB CALLS

Friday, March 8

PZC Commissioner George Courtney was quietly reading the evening paper when he was interrupted by the phone. He put aside his hot cup of lemon tea, a drink he enjoyed after dinner while reading and relaxing in his den. He placed his freshly lit cigarette in the nearby ashtray. Patting Bubba, his Golden Retriever on his head, he slowly picked up the phone. Bubba cocked his head, resentful of the intrusion with his master.

"George, this is Dominic Columbo, how ya doing?"

The tranquil relaxing mood that had engulfed George from the paper, tea, cigarette and Bubba was suddenly shattered. *What the hell is he calling me for?* "Hi Dom, what's up?" was all that George could muster up to the unwanted phone call. *Damn, I have to get caller ID.*

"I thought I'd give you a buzz to discuss the shopping center proposal. Lots of talk going on around the town on it. It's gonna be an important project for the town, don't you think?"

George said nothing.

Dominic continued. "You certainly are gonna have to make some tough decisions, especially after those agonizing public hearings. That was quite a show by that broad Burns, what a pain in the ass. Anyway I'd thought I'd give you a call to see if you wanted to talk about it; it being such an important proposal for Covingford."

None of your damn business George thought to himself but responded instead. "I'm already spending a lot of time reviewing the record and the facts on the proposal Dom. There was a lot of information presented at the hearing, and I wanna have a complete picture on the project before I make a decision. There are a lot of different viewpoints."

"I agree, George. That's why I calling."

Ignoring Dominic, George continued. "The Commission will be discussing it at a special meeting on the 18th, and then another special meeting right after that, hopefully to vote on it. Get this damn thing over. Why don't you come to the meetings and listen in. Unfortunately, since the hearings are over, we cannot take in any more information from the public, *including you*. Otherwise I'm sure the Commission would have loved to hear your views," George added with a touch of sarcasm. "Unfortunately you did not speak at the hearings. Come on down and listen to our debate. It should be an interesting discussion," George continued, rolling his eyes to Bubba, whose expression clearly reflected his annoyance at the sharing of his master's time.

"I might come down," replied Dominic, totally oblivious to the sarcasm. "I just thought I'd touch base with you prior to the meetings, since this is so important," Dominic continued, not missing a beat. "Me, Peter and Sal, we're very much in favor of it, and we all agree it will add so much to *our* community."

"As I said Dom, I have no conclusion on it at this time. I want to hear what the rest of the Commission has to say about it and weigh all the pros and cons. We are not supposed to have pre-disposed positions on it until *all* the facts are discussed and reviewed." George emphasized the word "all", feeling his blood pressure rise as his reply became more forceful. His right hand reached out and gently patted Bubba. The faithful dog's eyes told George that the phone call should end immediately, and that his master should get back to more important things. "We'll have a full debate on it and then render our opinion," George continued, as he watched the smoke from his cigarette lazily curl upward, its long ash of the un-smoked portion hanging in the ashtray.

"Understood," replied Dominic. "Just thought I'd touch base with you anyway. After all, you are in your second term already as a commissioner, and will be coming up again for re-appointment. You know how important the party's endorsement is."

The tone of Dominic's voice had changed just slightly, but George immediately picked it up. *Was it there - a threat? No, not quite, but still, something, something was there, something hidden. I really resent the tone of his last comment. What the hell is he getting at - that little bastard?*

"Dom, have to go. As I said, if you're that interested, come on down to the meetings and listen to our discussions. Talk to you later." George hung up the phone without waiting for a reply. His blood pressure had risen, and he could feel the tension throughout his body. His tranquility for the evening was shattered; his tea had gone cold, his cigarette burnt out. George kept repeating the conversation over and over in his mind as he stroked Bubba's long brown soft hair.

As much to Bubba as to himself, George hissed out loud "what was that reference to the party endorsement all about? I spoke to the political committee two years ago and gave them my back-ground and my views. I thought it went well. Damn, I've been en-dorsed twice by the committee for a seat on the PZC, no easy feat. And Dom's chair of the committee, he endorsed me. Now what? Did I miss something? Is there an agenda here I'm not aware of?"

Troubled, George tried to return to reading the paper, but the phone conversation and its innuendos kept coming back. The stories he had heard about Dominic further added to his discomfort. He reviewed every word he had said to Dominic and what Dominic had said to him, trying to figure out Dominic's angle and how he might turn it around. *If only I knew Dominic was going to call I could have been more prepared and guarded in my answers. His call came at the worst possible moment. Damn, I was so relaxed, it's been a long day. He really caught me off guard, what a pain in the ass, that fat oversized blimp. I should vote against the project just to spite him. It'd be fun to see him squirm.* "Damn, Damn, I hate politics," he murmured, "and I especially despise that little weasel."

Bubba, sensing his master's increased agitation, nuzzled him a little further and placed his head on lap. Looking up his eyes seemed to say, "Relax, I'm here. Don't let that little human bastard get to you."

Minutes later, Commissioner Jerry Katz's phone rang and his concern about another unpleasant conversation with Dominic Columbo came to fruition. Jerry still seethed every time he thought about the previous summer's encounter with the Bomb, although that encounter had taken place seven months earlier. It was a nightmare that just kept popping up in Jerry's mind. As he answered the phone and heard the voice, it was suddenly summer time again.

"Jerry, how are ya, this is Dominic, what's up?

"Hello Dominic, not much. What can I do for you?" Jerry abruptly replied. *Damn. Shoulda checked caller ID first.* He had vowed after last summer's experience with Dominic that if he ever spoke with him again, it would be curt and to the point. He was not going to get caught off guard again. He stood up from his easy chair, his entire body suddenly alert and tense. Holding his portable phone tightly to his ear, he walked into the kitchen, flicking on the overhead light as he entered. The glare of the light was in sharp contrast to the soft light next to his easy chair, where he had been totally immersed in his college's NCAA basketball game. The glaring overhead light contributed to his mood as his focus was now entirely on the phone conversation.

"I was just talk'n to a few people about the shopping center and I thought I'd give ya a call to discuss it," Dominic continued in a nonchalant tone. "After all, you are in the middle of the proposal and have an important say in the project. Any ideas on it at this point?"

Mind your own business you jerk. "No, not yet," Jerry could hear his voice rising. "As Commissioners we heard all of the evidence and next will discuss it. Then **we** will make a decision."

"Just thought you might want a little extra help, that's all."

"Public input is over. You ought to know that Dominic, you've been around for a while. You had your chance at the hearing," Jerry threw in, hoping to put the Bomb a little bit on the defensive. Pacing around the kitchen, Jerry noticed the thermometer on the outside of the kitchen window, the red mercury settling in on the bottom as the temperature hovered around 20. He contrasted this to himself as he had a quick flashback to the summer barbecue with its warmth and bright sunshine, until Dominic had come into his face. *Summer or winter, doesn't matter, this guy's always a pain in the ass.*

"Well, I just wanted to touch base with ya since it's such an important project for our town," Dominic continued, ignoring the dig about knowing zoning procedures. "It's going to add quite a bit to the tax base, and will offer a lot of employment, especially for teenagers. Gee Jerry, as I recall, isn't your daughter 16 now? I bet she is going to be looking for a nice part-time job for after school, don't ya think?"

If Jerry could have reached through the phone and grabbed Dominic's throat at that moment, he would have done so, regardless of the consequences. The reference to his daughter brought an angry flush to his face. His hand tightened on the phone, which, if it were not made of unbreakable plastic, would have been squeezed like an over ripe banana. "Look Dominic, I gotta go. Come to the meeting on the 18th, and listen to our debates. You might learn something," *although I doubt it*. Without a goodbye, he slammed the phone down. His evening, like that of Commissioner Courtney's, was in shambles.

Dominic sat back in his oversize worn black leather chair. He felt worried, pleased and excited, all at the same time. He took a long drag on his cigar, and slowly blew out several perfect rings of smoke, a trick he had developed with years of practice. He reflected on his phone calls. He had immediately sensed the tension and agitation in both George's and Jerry's tones. "Those two are more than a little defensive, must be something in their past that's bothering them," he chuckled to himself and looked down at Snowball, who gazed lovingly up at him. "Too bad," Dom continued as he looked intently at Snowball, "I'm sure they will now give this project a full objective consideration." Snowball's bedroom eyes blinked softly in concurrence. Dom was worried however. The lack of a commitment from the two commissioners bothered Dominic. The more he thought about the conversation, especially with Jerry, the more worried he became. Jerry had been so evasive, why? The project had to pass. Dominic dreaded the consequences if it failed. Louie the Enforcer had left no doubt on Dominic's future - or lack thereof- if the shopping center was turned down.

Dominic slowly struggled up from his chair, not an easy task. All of these worries made him hungry. He waddled into the kitchen and opened the freezer, his appetite whetted for a huge scoop of chocolate chip ice cream with hot chocolate sauce melted over it. "A good sedative," he said aloud, "One more Commissioner to call, and that will be it for tonight. Marilyn Erickson. She's going to be tough. It's too bad Jim Bradley is so independent, that's probably why he is chairman of the Commission. I'm not sure how I'm going to handle him. At least if he were a Democrat or a Republican, I could bring some pressure on him. Fuckin independent! Maybe Sal or Peter can come up with an angle. Anyway, time to focus on something more immediate," he grinned, removing from the microwave the hot thick chocolate sauce he just heated up. Slowly he poured it over the large mounds of Ben and Jerry's extra rich creamy chocolate chip ice cream. "Yes, a little dab of whipped cream just gives it the right touch. Hmm, there are some things in life that have to have a priority" he continued in a loud voice to no one but himself and Snowball, who sat patiently waiting for a taste.

Having built up his strength with the snack, Dominic made his third phone call that evening to Marilyn Erickson, a member of the Commission for over six years. A mid-level manager in Anthem's Blue Cross's headquarters, she was known as a no nonsense administrator. A mother of four children, she knew the antics that children played and the excuses that they used. She brought to the Commission her skills as an administrator and a mother. Although sometimes perceived as being abrupt, people knew very quickly where they stood with her. Dominic was aware of this, and thus he made her his last call of that evening, able to put it off no longer. He slowly dialed.

"Hello Dominic, what do you want?" Marilyn's military tone threw Dominic off.

The abruptness of her greeting and then her silence made Dominic all the more uneasy.

"I, I, just wanted to talk to you about the shopping center and its importance. . . "

"Hold it right there Dominic. The hearing is over. You know that. No more input."

"Yeah, but this is key to. . . "

"What part of my conversation don't you understand? The hearing is over, *period*."

"But I . . . "

"Dominic, I am a busy person. If there is nothing else to this conversation than the shopping center, our discussion is over."

"No . . . no, that was it." Dominic stumbled over the words, trying to figure out how she got him on the defensive so fast.

"Then goodbye, Dominic, have a nice night." The line went dead.

Dominic stared at his phone, flabbergasted. In less than 20 seconds he'd been blown off, and by a broad to boot! *Glad I'm not married to her, holy shit!* Slowly he put the phone down, still trying to figure how she had controlled the conversation so quickly.

Dialing up Sal's number, he could feel his blood pressure rising. "Sal, this is Dom. I just spoke to the three commissioners on the shopping center."

"How did it go?" Sal inquired, knowing Dominic had his own way of dealing with people, sometimes quite successfully.

"I'm, I'm not sure," he stuttered into the phone.

"What do you mean you're not sure? You know what's riding on this." Sal exploded over the phone.

"I, I reminded George Courtney about the importance of center to the town's tax base and the fact that . . ."

"Did you remind him that he got our party's endorsement for the PZC seat he holds?

"I did, but he wasn't interested in discussing it."

"People have short memories. Anyway, which way is he leaning"?

"He wouldn't say. Still thinking about it, but I think he is in favor."

"Hmmm. What about Katz?"

"He wasn't too happy to hear from me. I reminded him of our conversation last summer about his little visit from our police department. I think he is still very nervous about the incident and that it still might come out in public. I did emphasize our position on this project."

"Good," Sal replied. "And what about the Primadonna?" Sal's favorite term for Marilyn Erickson.

"What a bitch. That broad blew me off. I couldn't even get to first base."

"I'm not surprised. She is tough. She is a little too independent. I can have Peter give her a call," Sal offered.

"Ok by me. I don't want to deal with her."

"I'll call Councilor Mitchell and see how he's making out with the Commissioners he was gonna call. He was also going to have some of the other Council members make some calls and try and line up votes. I know he was really concerned after that large public turnout at the hearing. Damn letters to the editor—and now those goddam lawn signs. Crazy. No one expected that."

"That's for sure. Have Mitchell remind Commissioner Wiggins that his brother-in-law works for public works and he had a little help several years ago in securing that position," Dominic said.

"I forgot about that. Might be a good card to play."

"Yeah, that's what I think. We need all the help we can get, that's for sure. We underestimated this one. It's these damn broads. First it was that neighborhood housewife who organized that group."

"Marcia Richards, a pain in the ass.""

"Yeah, that's her. Then they hired that short-skirted Attorney Burns, and she really got the pot boiling. I know what she could use."

"Save it."

"Yeah, but did you notice it's the broads that are screwing up this proposal. What's going wrong in our society?"

"We'll know shortly. The Commission's meeting in the next few weeks, and then will decide. So we gotta move on this even more."

"Ok Sal, I'll continue to explore our resources and see what else pops up."

"Talk to you later Dom." Sal hung up, knowing that Dom's "popping up" could mean more embarrassing information on certain people. *What a memory that guy has! It's a good thing. We're gonna need everything he's got for this one.*

Chapter 15
THE BOMB AND THE ENFORCER

TUESDAY, MARCH 12

"Your IOUs are climbing again Dominic, even higher than last time." The threatening voice sent chills down Dominic's spine as he sat in the small room opposite Louie the Enforcer. The phone call to Dominic's cell phone shortly before had been curt and direct—"Dominic, we need to talk, NOW. Meet me in the New Haven office in two hours." The line went dead before Dominic had a chance to even respond.

The room Dominic reluctantly found himself in was on the third floor in downtown New Haven, just off Whitney Avenue. It was an early 1900's house that had been converted to three levels of offices, the first two floors housed legitimate operations - or fairly legitimate operations. The sign on the front of the building identified the small law offices on the first and second floors. No sign identified the office on the third floor or even made any mention of it. It was there for whomever needed office space, by the week, day or just an hour. No questions asked, cash up front was all that was needed. The owner of the building rented out the room, cash only, on a regular basis, knowing that his clients were not interested in signs out front. The lower law offices, busy with their own practices, paid little attention to the changing clients and traffic on the third floor.

The Bomb knew that the Enforcer was no one to fool with. The enforcer's nickname had been justly earned, not just given to him. Stories about his enforcement methods for underworld characters were well known. Rumor had it that he even caused a minister to have an "accident" resulting in a broken arm and several dislocated fingers. Dominic had heard all the stories, and whether or not they were true, his imagination ran wild whenever Louie's name came up. Not a character to mess with. And now here he was, sitting less than three feet from Dominic, eye-ball to eye-ball. Dominic's stomach tightened, matching the inner core of a golf ball; his intestines gurgled inside his three hundred pounds. He broke out in a sweat. His recent brush with Louie, or at least his glove, was still fresh in his memory. After all, it was just two weeks ago in the school parking lot after the public hearing on the shopping center. He vividly remembered the glove as it clamped fiercely over his mouth when he had entered his cold car. Now the same feeling of fear was back.

"I know. I know. I've had a terrible run of bad luck, terrible." Dominic replied, the fear in his throat rising. Despite the coolness of the room, sweat started to drip from his forehead.

"Touching, so sad," replied the Enforcer in a sarcastic tone. Louie stared at Dominic, *just another stupid gambler, a big fat stupid one at that.*

Louie's body language and tone clearly conveyed to Dominic that he could care less about Dom's run of "bad luck." The Bomb said nothing, just sat there, waiting, his parched throat failing to work. He could feel his heart start to race.

"You got lucky last time when your in-laws bailed you out," the Enforcer continued. "I understand that's not going to happen again this time." He cupped his hand as he lit his cigarette and blew a cloud of smoke into Dominic's face. He watched the Blimp squint and push back in his chair, a look of terror on his face.

"No, no they can't. My wife tells me her parents have no more money," Dominic barely got the last few words out, his throat dry and scratchy. He gasped for air, trying to avoid the smoke that seemed to hang over him like the cloud in the cartoon character Joe Btfspik in Al Capp's Li'l Abner. He looked into the menacing eyes staring back at him, the steel cold dark eyes of the Enforcer, an unflinching, menacing hard stare. Dominic shuddered. Louie just sat there, puffing away on his cigarette, smoke spewing out through his nostrils. Dominic focused on the cigarette, a lump in his throat.

"My employer is not happy at all with the reports they got on the turnout at the public hearing on the shopping center. They have a lot of money invested in this application," the Enforcer continued. "An awful lot of people are suddenly against this project. Letters to the editor, signs on front lawns, people waving signs on street corners telling drivers to honk if they are against the project, and it is getting noisy!" he continued menacingly. "And according to today's Inquirer's report, the Commission is meeting NEXT Monday to discuss and possibly vote on the project. Let's hope that the Commissioners are not waffling. This was supposed to be a slam dunk." To Dominic's amazement, Louie's cigarette dangled even further. The room went quiet, the late afternoon sun pierced through the dirty yellowing windows, illuminating millions of dust particles that seemed to dance throughout the room.

"The neighbors, they, they just organized faster than what I expected – faster than what anyone expected," Dominic forced out, still fixated on the cigarette's angle, despite his overwhelming anxiety.

"We pay you to anticipate these items. What happened to your local hotshot Attorney Cimione? He didn't deliver at the hearing. You recommended him. Matter of fact, that female attorney Burns fuckin blew him out of the water."

"He got blindsided by that bitch, she came outta nowhere. She really got the crowd wound up, caught us off balance. . ."

"Cut the excuses," snapped the Enforcer. " We pay for results, and . . ." with a dark sinister grin spreading across his face, "We also collect when there are no results."

Dominic sat there frozen in place. The sweat burned his eyes but he did not move. Visions of more stories of Louie the Enforcer flashed through his mind.

"What's happening with your contacts on the Planning and Zoning Commission? You're always bragging you have dirt on everybody," Louie continued.

"I made several phone calls over the weekend, and the Commissioners are being non-committal. They see the value of the project to the town, but there is some concern over the impact on the neighborhood. I have one Commissioner though that I am sure will vote in favor of the project. I already called him, and let me just say, he wasn't too happy to hear from me. I reminded him of the discussion we had last summer on a little traffic incident that never made the news, it kinda got covered up." Dominic briefly smiled as he thought about his recent conversation with Katz and how he was really shaken up by the call. He certainly had not been happy to be reminded of the conversation about the drunken driving incident. "Yes," Dominic said with more conviction then he felt, "we definitely have his affirmative vote, so only two more needed, a simple majority of the five member commission. And we think we got the other two votes, making three. That's all we need. And watch the newspapers for some more letters to the editor supporting the project. Me and the Garganos are working full time on this."

"We're running out of time, Dominic. Get your fat ass in gear."

"No problem, no problem. We are all working on it. It's gonna fly."

"It better."

"Gotta ask you though. There's some stories floating around about contamination of the property," Dominic said, trying to gain his composure and shift the conversation away from his own failures. "You guys assured me that you had taken care of the tests."

"We did take care of them. The test borings were taken in very selected places and the report sanitized before it was published. Nobody can prove otherwise. It's a signed and notarized environmental report. Real formal and legal, just like the attorneys love." He smiled at his reference to the attorneys taking care of legal reports.

"But I'm telling ya Louie, stories are starting to float around about some kinda contamination from a long time ago. Even pain-in-the-ass Janet Johnson is poking her nose into it." The cloud of smoke still hung over Dominic's head.

"Shit. All we need now is that broad poking her newspaper nose into this." Louie's tone suddenly changed, a hint of worry. The last thing he and his employers wanted was a reporter poking around into the project, especially Janet Johnson. He heard she had lots of contacts, and she just might trip over something. "What info does she have?"

"She called one of the neighbors near the site the other day and was asking questions about whether the kids in the area play in there."

"And?"

"The neighbor was somewhat evasive, said the kids had other areas to play in that were better."

"Smart answer. How did you hear about it?"

"The neighbor is an old gambling friend of mine. Said he did not want to say too much. He's concerned that if anything got into the papers about contamination in the area, it might ruin the value of his property since he lives close by." Dominic watched the cigarette as it reached the point of almost burning Louie's lip.

"This project's gotta fly. There is too much money at stake here, including the forgiving of the measly 100g's gambling debt you owe. As soon as the PZC approves of the project, my employer is set to exercise his option and close on the land. Then building starts," Louie said.

"But if it's contaminated, what will happen?" Dominic asked, suddenly curious himself on how this would work.

"We'll just pave over every square inch," Louie replied as he removed the last burning ember of his cigarette. He threw it on the floor and squashed it with his shoe. *Always pays to be careful.* "The paving will cover a lot of stuff, keep it buried. That's why this project is so compact with the anchor store and all the smaller stores bunched together. Everything is going to get covered over with pavement between the parking lots and the buildings." A look of pride seemed to come over Louie as he explained the cover up.

"Won't they have any plantings and landscaping?" Dominic asked.

"Sure, lots of it. They'll bring in their own soil, nice and clean. The place will appear green as can be. Flowers, bushes, trees, you name it. Terrific landscaping. Even some of the mature trees on the site will stay, for historic sake. The environmentalists will love it. Give awards, plaques, speeches, the whole nine yards," Louie continued with a laugh. "Public water will supply the place, so nobody gets hurt, clean pure drinking water. Not like the drinking water debacle they had in Flint Michigan," he added sarcastically.

"So what happens with the contamination?" Dominic sat up in his chair, suddenly wondering what he had gotten into.

"Covered over, buried." Louie replied nonchalantly. "Maybe sometime in the future when we are all outta here something might surface. Look at how long it took for the Love Canal chemical contamination to be found out."

"That was in New York, wasn't it?"

"Yeah, in the 70's. Contamination of chemical waste by industry for years. Eventually the land was sold and a nice pretty subdivision built on the land. Over a hundred houses built, lawns, flowers, even a school. Suburbia, USA. It took years before the slimy black ooze started coming out of the land. A newspaper reporter got a Pulitzer Prize for his investigation of the site. Even the Feds got involved."

"Cripes, I remember the stories about that place, high numbers of cancer and other bad health issues. Is this land that bad?" Dominic's eyes bulged as he asked in incredulous tone.

"Nah. This land is nowhere near that, just a little midnight contamination 30 years ago or so."

"Contamination of what?"

"You're starting to get a little too nosy Dominic. Just focus on your efforts on getting approval and don't worry, this is not Love Canal. Just remember, you're already in this up to your triple chin."

Dominic shivered uncontrollably. It was dawning on him just how serious the contamination of the land could be. A piece of trivia he had not bothered with before; it wasn't his project. He was just helping Covingford out, promoting economic development. Suddenly the extent of the proposal hit him. "Could the Feds get involved with this?" he asked with a quivering voice.

"Dom, don't get excited. But since you ask, did you ever hear of the Superfund."

"Holy shit. That's those federal monies for big contaminated areas. That's big stuff. Heavy duty." Dominic's eyes almost popped out of his head.

"Yeah, yeah, but don't worry, if the FBI comes in and investigates, you'll only get twenty years or so," Louie said with a smirk.

The joking about the seriousness of the situation was lost on Dominic. His whole body started to shiver, like three hundred pounds of Jell-O on a vibrator, every wrinkle shaking to its own beat. "The FBI." The words struck terror in Dominic. Why had he run up those gambling debts, where was it leading him to now? For the first time Dominic realized he was in over his head, way over his head. His body shook even more, as though caught in a Richter 7 earthquake.

Louie watched Dominic's face go pale, even Dominic's chair was shaking. "Look Dominic, don't worry," Louie offered, recognizing that Dominic was near the edge. "You've made your phone calls, so just stay on top of things. Do any last minute stuff you have to do insure at least the 3 votes and everything will be fine. That's all we need is 3 votes. Bingo! The project gets built, Garganos get the construction work, the town gets tax revenue, the dump is cleaned up, and, best of all, your gambling debts disappear. A win-win for everyone," he added with a wry smile.

"But, but, what happens if the vote fails?" Dominic asked in a half pleading, half mournful voice.

"In that case Mr. Bomb," Louie looked directly into Dominic's eyes which were now wide open, pushing out through the layers of fat in the eyelids and in the cheeks. "In that case," the Enforcer reiterated in a deep sinister tone, "the FBI might then be viewed by you as the friendlies."

Tuesday March 12
PZC Handles Backlog
Shopping Center Discussion Delayed
By Janet Johnson
Inquirer Staff Reporter

The Planning and Zoning Commission met last night to catch up on their backlog caused by the lengthy process of dealing with the proposed shopping center. Several routine applications were discussed and acted upon. The proposed shopping center was not on the agenda.

The Commission will meet again on Monday, the 18th, and the only item on that agenda will be a discussion and possible vote on the proposal by Pilgrim Enterprises to construct a new shopping center on 25 acres of vacant land in the southeast section of Covingford. The proposal has generated a considerable amount of controversy. Public input on the shopping center will not be allowed at next week's meeting since the hearings have been officially closed.

Two weeks ago the Commission held several nights of public hearings which were loud and noisy as both sides presented their views in a stimulating debate. The Commission meeting last night was only to address their backlog of business. The Commission's role now is to study the information that was entered into the record at those hearings, and make its decision, which by law must be done within 65 days of the hearings closure, which was February 27th. State Statutes require the PZC to only consider the information in the original proposal and what was presented at the public hearings. Thus the Commission cannot allow any further discussion from the public at its meetings.

The final night of the hearings became quite heated. A neighborhood group, called SWAT, was organized by resident Marcia Richards. They had hired an attorney, Patricia Burns, to represent them. The neighborhood is dead set against the new proposal, citing traffic and a total disruption of lifestyle both to their neighborhood and to the town itself.

Next week's PZC meeting will be held in the Town Council Chambers at 7:00.

Chapter 16

THE TOWN MANAGER'S REPORT ON THE PROJECT

MEMO: Covingford Town Council
FROM: Kurt Thomas, Town Manager
RE: Fiscal Analysis of Proposed Retail Shopping Center
DATE: March 15

Per the Town Council's request, attached please find the requested fiscal analysis of the proposed retail center by Pilgrim Enterprises. This report was prepared mostly in-house, but some technical outside assistance was provided by the firm Economic Development Consultants (EDC), which specializes in these types of reports. This was per my request.

The Council had requested this fiscal analysis to illustrate the impact the proposal would have on the Town's finances. The attached report covers this economic impact. However, in light of the myriad questions raised at the Planning and Zoning Commission's public hearings, I have also added another section which addresses some of the environmental and other issues raised at the hearings by the adjacent neighbors.

In brief, the proposal will have a positive effect on Covingford in three major ways: construction, retail jobs, and property tax revenue.

Construction: The initial phase, construction activity, will help the Town inasmuch as we have residents who, as skilled tradesmen, could be employed over the next two years. These individuals would be employed by the construction or general contractor. I am suggesting, in the event the PZC approves of the project, that the Council call the developer in for a lengthy discussion on several items, including giving local residents preference in the developer's hiring practices for the construction phase. Hopefully the stores that eventually come in will employ our local residents. We also need to discuss with the developers several other items.

This employment factor will be significant, and it will then have secondary fiscal impacts as money is spent on other services. This is the multiplier effect, as money is then spent on groceries, restaurants, amusements, home appliances, and even cars. Covingford does have existing businesses that can provide all of these items. The scale of the project and the estimated length of construction time of approximately 2-3 years insure the influx of several millions of dollars into the local economy fairly quickly.

The Council does have jurisdiction over the developer in several areas, such as: is the developer interested in having the main entrance road be a town road; storm drainage connections outside of the development itself; and hooking up to the Town's water and sewer system. As noted, all of these items fall under the jurisdiction of the Town Council and will require the Council's approval.

Retail jobs: The second phase of the project, the opening and operation of the stores, will provide a steady stream of employment, again benefiting the local economy. Based on the developer's projections, it is estimated that over 500 full and part-time positions will be created. Inasmuch as most of these positions will be retail and service jobs, it is reasonable to assume most will be taken by local residents due to the cost of commuting. Nonetheless, this employment level should be substantial, and would positively reduce Covingford's current 6% unemployment rate. The developers project that the annual payroll impact will be in the range of $12,000,000 to $18,000,000, a major plus to the Town. Then, again, the multiplier effect kicks in, which economists estimate to be in the 3-5 times range. This is very significant!

The new shopping center will certainly increase Covingford's visibility in the State, and could even increase tourism to our local historic sites. This certainly will please our Historical Society.

Property tax revenue: The third level will be the direct increase of tax revenue to the Town. As our Economic Development Commissioners testified at the first night of the zoning hearings, there will be a substantial increase in property tax revenue. The project is anticipated to increase our Grand List, or amount of taxable property, by $70-80 million. Using our current assessment and mill (taxation) rate, this would generate an additional ANNUAL $1.5 to $2 million in new tax revenue. This will have a positive direct impact on our tax base, and will assist the Town in not only controlling our taxation rate, but give us some breathing room to address some long standing problems, not the least of which is the renovation of Covingford's high school, which was built in 1974. Another ancillary impact may be higher tax revenue generated from newer cars, which are also subject to the annual property tax rate (this is not true in many other states).

Thus, all three phases of this proposal: construction, retail jobs, and property tax revenue, are all very positive for Covingford and something the Town desperately needs. These phases will be significant, and for the most part, positive.

Other: However, on the other side of the coin, is the impact on the environment and on the neighborhoods. As was brought out in the hearings, the adjacent residential neighborhood may be adversely impacted. The constant flow of traffic-construction, shoppers, employees, and service trucks will overwhelm the local road system and directly impact the quality of life of the neighborhood residents. We anticipate a lowering of the real estate values in the area. The quality of life, a factor impossible to quantify, could possibly be adverse. Children in the neighborhood currently use the local streets for bike riding and even playing games. (A few of the cul-de-sacs even have permanent basketball hoops set up on them!). Part of this problem could be ameliorated by the construction of new parks in the area, albeit at an additional cost to the town.

Noise is another major element. Currently, the adjacent neighborhood has been described as a quiet residential area. This will change with the substantial increase in truck and car traffic, and this change will be permanent. In the construction phase, the constant flow of heavy equipment through the neighborhood will no doubt be substantial, especially since construction is estimated to take 2-3 years. If it turns out there is substantial ledge in the area, blasting will be required. This will involve a pre-blasting evaluation of the homes before construction can start. There will be a considerable aggravation factor associated with this, both for the residents and for the developer.

Furthermore, the increase in traffic will impact air quality due not only to the increase in cars and trucks, but due to the loss of trees on the site. The site, as we all know, is heavily overgrown with trees and shrubs.

Further discussion and analysis could be undertaken to evaluate the possibility of only one main entrance road to the site with a secondary emergency exit. The Town may require stiff local traffic controls for the area immediately outside of the development, such as traffic calming measures (curved roads, landscaping in the road, stop signs, etc.). The costs of these improvements will be subject to negotiations with the developer and the town, but again, only if initial approval is granted by the Planning and Zoning Commission.

Conclusion: The proposal will have a very positive impact on the finances of Covingford as a whole, but at the same time, have an adverse effect on the adjacent neighborhood. Employment opportunities will increase. It is important to note that the extent of this neighborhood impact could be somewhat mitigated through positive action by the Town, such as the construction of new parks, heavy landscaping, and improvements to the road system, although these would be costly to the Town. At the appropriate time, I do expect our Town Planner and Town Engineer to provide recommendations on noise and traffic remediation techniques, such as sound barriers, landscaping, screening, and buffering to help mitigate noise, traffic congestions, and visual disturbances. However, there will be significant changes from the undeveloped state the land is currently in.

Per the Town Council's standard procedure, the attached financial report will appear on the Town Council's next agenda for review and discussion. This advanced copy is being provided just to the Town Council per the direction of Keith Mitchell. I do anticipate the press will be requesting copies of the report as soon as they hear about it, which, based on past experience, will be very shortly, and before the Council's next scheduled meeting.

Please advise if there are any questions or anything else the Councilors will want to add.

Thank you.

———

Kurt sat back and stared at his computer screen. The hot coffee mug felt good in his hands and the caffeine perked him up. As he reread his memo, he realized it did go beyond the requested fiscal analysis, but he felt it was important to keep the proposal in perspective. And, if the PZC did give approval, he wanted to be sure the Council knew the major role it would then have on the project and the surrounding neighborhood. *All important information for the Council, but I bet Councilor Mitchell won't be too thrilled with the additional information. He's a hard one to figure out, never sure where he is going or what he is up to.*

Kurt paused over the send button, just one stroke to send the memo to the Town Council. He hesitated, realizing his memo would stir things up, especially with Mitchell, but he felt strongly he had to say what he said. *Happy St. Patrick's Day* he mused to himself. As he pondered, he opened his file drawer to review some of the prior news articles on the project. As a matter of course, he kept files of published news articles on important topics facing the town. It helped him stay on top of the issues, as well as often providing insight into items that seemed insignificant at the time. In perusing the articles, one letter to the editor jumped out at him.

The letter had been sent in almost two months ago, early on in the project when it was first publically announced. Kurt had read it originally and filed it, but in rereading it now in light of the hearings and the neighborhood opposition, it carried more significance. The author was a native of the town, born, raised, and educated locally, and except for four years away at college, had returned to Covingford to marry a local girl and continue to live in town. Kurt was always amazed at how many people did this, always returning, or staying, in the town where they were born and raised, and would never think of leaving. He laughed to himself when he recalled talking with one such resident about the life of a Town Manager. Kurt had been working for a town in the New Haven area about 30 miles away, and had commuted for a year before selling his house and moving to Covingford. The man had expressed utter amazement at the commuting distance that Kurt had to travel. The man even went on to say that he seldom visited that part of the State and knew little about New Haven, other than Yale was there and there were good pizza joints on Wooster Street. Kurt recalled feeling like a nomad after that conversation, having worked for various towns both in and out of Connecticut.

He smiled as he re-read the letter from the Covingford native.

January 16
EDITORIAL PAGE
THE INQUIRER

Let's Move Quickly

Regarding the new shopping center proposal, we need to move quickly to approve this plan before we lose this fantastic opportunity! The plan has nothing but benefits. And if we miss this chance, who knows what will happen next with this current dumpsite. The PZC will be holding hearings next month at the end of February.

The property is currently owned by the Alder Family Trust. When my old friend Sam Alder died some 30 years ago, the family created the trust until they could decide what to do. Over the years nothing ever happened except that the area filled in with trash blown in by storms (and I'd guess in some cases trash was dumped there in the middle of the night by unknown residents or even worse by folks from outside town). The result is an eyesore.

If Pilgrim's plan is approved by the Town, I understand they have agreed to buy the land and immediately begin developing it per their plan. If it isn't approved, who knows what will happen. Maybe nothing. Maybe it will just stay there as the eyesore it is now till the trust decides what to do with it. They don't seem to pay much attention to it since they all live out of state. Who knows how long that will take? And who knows what the next plan will be? Maybe not even as good as this one!

As they say, "the devil you know is always better than the one you don't know"!

Our town is over 200 years old. It's time for some new thinking. Change is inevitable so let's get the best deal we can while we can. This plan will do just that, so let's seize this opportunity and move forward just as fast as we can. Increased tax revenue, more jobs-a no brainer. We may not get a better chance—or even ANOTHER chance- anytime soon. Let's all support this proposal.

Frank Shepard
Covingford

Kurt re-read the phrase, "and I'd guess in some cases trash was dumped there in the middle of the night by unknown residents or even worse by folks from outside town." *Night time dumping?* He straightened up immediately in his chair. *How had he overlooked that?* That wording in that January letter had been insignificant at the time, but now, in light of what was coming out, perhaps there was more to this proposal than meets the eye. *I wonder if Janet has any more information on this? Could be very significant if the project does get approved, especially with the amount of paving and buildings planned for the project. Almost the entire area will be covered over. I better call Janet to see if she has more details, and perhaps, even more important, the town attorney.*

Kurt paused for another moment. Decision time.

He hit the "Send" button on his computer.

Chapter 17
THE PZC MEETING

Monday, March 18

"It now being 7:00 o'clock, this meeting will come to order," announced Chairman Jim Bradley. "We have a quorum since all five members of the Commission are present. Tonight's meeting is a special meeting with only one item on the agenda, the proposal by Pilgrim Enterprises for a new shopping center in the southeast section of Covingford. I see we have well over 40 residents here tonight, as well as the attorneys representing both sides. I would remind everyone that inasmuch as the public hearings are officially closed, no citizen input will be allowed. Only the Commission members can speak."

"I thought we lived in a democracy," one resident groused. Several members of the public sitting next to him murmured their concurrence. The little old lady in the front just nodded her head and continued her knitting non-stop; she took in every word with an all-knowing look on her aging face.

Ignoring the resident's comment, Bradley continued. "At the end of our discussions, the Commission may vote on the project, although the Commission has until May 3rd or approximately six more weeks to make its decision. To start things off, does any member of the Commission wish to speak?"

Bradley looked at each commissioner, and the discussion started.

"I think the proposal will greatly improve that run down area. It's been abandoned for a long time, a real eye sore. The proposal fits the land. Pilgrim had done a nice job with its land use plan and internal traffic circulation. They even addressed the small wetlands piece on the northern corner with their new drainage system. This will be great for Covingford. Overall, I'm really impressed," concluded one member.

A collective groan emerged from the audience, several feet began to shuffle. Attorney Cimione, seated in the front row, said nothing but took several notes. Attorney Burns, sitting behind him with the neighborhood group, said nothing but also scribbled some notes. After all, both were on the clock and had to show something to support their upcoming bills to their clients. Reporter Janet Johnson also scribbled furiously, taking notes almost verbatim. She had previously placed her small recorder on the table where the Commission was seated, wanting to insure she got every spoken word correct. She was pleased that the circulation of her paper had jumped significantly since the public hearings, and not one criticism suggesting a misquote. Her editor had been duly impressed with the number of letters to the editor that were being sent in almost daily, a sure sign not only of the increased readership, but of the intensity of the proposal.

"I'm not so sure. I strongly disagree! "retorted Commissioner Erickson. "Look at the impact on the residents that live around the project. The additional traffic will devastate their neighborhood. How would you like to live next to this proposed site?" she challenged her fellow Commissioner with angry penetrating eyes.

"Let's stay on the subject and not get into arguing with one another," Bradley chided. Both members glared at each other but did not challenge the Chair. The Town Planner and Town Engineer were then asked several questions about the traffic pattern and the proposed development configuration.

The commissioners debated the pros and cons of the project for the next five hours, and the weary public followed every comment. An occasional groan or a whispered "unbelievable" floated thru the air from the audience. No one left the meeting except for the 10 minute bathroom recess.

"This Commission certainly is divided and good points have been made on each side. Land use, traffic, taxes, employment, road circulation, building heights, wetlands, even pedestrian walkways, very comprehensive discussions. Impressive. I think we are getting close to a formal vote since we are starting to repeat our arguments. I suggest that we adjourn our meeting as it is almost midnight and meet next week to continue discussions and hopefully take a formal vote. That will give us time to mull over all the discussions we had tonight. I think we are close to a vote. We have reviewed a lot of items. Agreed?"

The exhausted Commissioners all nodded their weary heads in agreement, welcoming the end of the marathon session, and the additional delay in the actual vote. The audience sat silently, carefully listening to every word, watching the proceedings, and analyzing the body language of each commissioner.

Following a motion, a second, and a weary vote, Bradley announced, "Meeting adjourned till next Monday night the 25th at 7:00. Please be prepared to vote then, although we do have additional time for further discussion if needed." The members closed their notebooks, thoroughly drained, and quietly left the meeting. The atmosphere was in stark contrast to the last night of the public hearings just a few short weeks previously. Several citizens stayed around to talk with one another and with Attorney Burns. Attorney Cimione quietly left the meeting. Both attorneys realized that they generated five billable hours without saying a word.

COVINGFORD'S PZC DEBATES
SHOPPING CENTER PROPOSAL
Tuesday March 19
By Janet Johnson
Inquirer Staff Reporter

COVINGFORD – Last night the Covingford Planning and Zoning Commission met for almost five hours, adjourning at midnight, to discuss the pending proposal for a shopping center in town. This was the second public meeting of the Commission since the contentious public hearings almost three weeks ago. Last week the Commission met to catch up on their backlog of other applications and did not discuss the proposed Pilgrim development. Chairman Bradley reminded the residents at last night's meeting that "no further public input can be taken on the shopping center since the public hearings were over."

The Commission members exhaustedly debated several points on the proposal, asking several times for staff input on questions involving land configuration and traffic impact on the adjacent neighborhood. At times the debate became quite vocal and strident. Toward the end of the marathon session, members, clearly fatigued, began rehashing points made hours earlier. A simple majority of the Commission or three affirmative votes of the five members are required for approval. Although no vote was taken, the Commission members appear deeply divided on the proposal.

Members of the public expressed frustration on their inability to participate. "I thought we lived in a Democracy," resident Ray Kowalski said after the meeting. "Damn, we couldn't even talk at the meeting. All we could do was listen, and listen we did, for five long hours."

Chairman Bradley stated the Commission will hold another special meeting on March 25th to discuss and possibly vote on the shopping center. The Commissioners appeared ready to take a vote at the end of last night's marathon meeting. The Commission has to vote within 65 days of the hearings, which closed February 27.

March 19
Letters to the Editor
The Inquirer

Approve this Oasis

As a senior citizen and life-long resident of Covingford, I WRITE IN SUPPORT OF THE Pilgrim Enterprise plan to develop a new shopping center near my home in Covingford. It will help the town by bringing in several popular retail stores and I'm told will also add 600 jobs, most of which will likely go to town residents. Just imagine how much tax revenue will come to the town and how much more money will flow into the town's economy as a result. Those benefits are very important to me since I live on a fixed income and watch with deep concern the ever increasing tax burden here in town and in this state.

The new complex will be beautifully landscaped and from pictures I've seen it will look like an oasis. There will be no impact on my neighborhood—if I thought there would be, I'd stay silent or even oppose it since I live just up the street. I think it will likely even <u>increase</u> the value of my house since I'll be in walking distance of the new stores. And what do we lose? NOTHING! Instead of a trash filled eyesore that's been a dumping ground for years, we'll have a beautiful new modern shopping center with a great new grocery store. It will be a showcase and an asset to the town.

I urge my friends, the members of the Planning and Zoning Commission, to quickly approve this plan as soon as possible.

Ingrid Conners
Covingford

EDITORIAL PAGE
THE INQUIRER
March 20

EDITOR'S NOTE: *The Inquirer* had been deluged with letters to the editor on the proposed shopping center in Covingford since the Planning and Zoning Commission held public hearings on the project at the end of February. In light of the intense interest in this project, the paper's editorial staff has selected several letters sent to us for publication, both pro and con, and our editorial staff thus devotes this page to these letters. All letters are from Covingford residents.

Failing Infrastructure Needs Attention Numerous residents of Covingford have recently expressed their views on why the new shopping center proposal should be approved. We couldn't agree more!

It's no secret that our town infrastructure is crumbling before our eyes. It's common knowledge that the high school is in a sad state of disrepair. Years of neglect and limited maintenance have caused serious problems like leaks, heating inefficiencies and other issues. In winter, students have to wear coats to class all day. It's almost impossible to hold summer classes since many classroom windows are sealed shut. And anyone who attended the recent hearings knows that the cafeteria turned into a sauna due to ineffective heating and ventilation. Unfortunately, other town buildings are in the same serious situation due to neglect and deferred maintenance. Town Hall and the high school both need major work.

We have this wonderful shopping center plan which will bring in millions of dollars in new tax revenue for many years. It may also provide new part time jobs for youth like our sons, for seniors in need of a few extra dollars, and many others including the unfortunate unemployed and others here in town. It's obviously a solution to the problems we face and for the life of me I can't see ANY reason why we haven't fully embraced the plan and approved it wholeheartedly and without reservation. We should listen to these wise neighbors and

all support approval of the Pilgrim Enterprise plan.

Eric and Emily Foreman

Destruction of Quiet Area- Vote NO
In the next few weeks the Town PZC will vote on the Pilgrim Enterprises redevelopment project. THEY SHOULD VOTE NO!! This plan would allow an out of town developer with no ties to the community to build an unneeded shopping center in a very quiet residential part of our beautiful town.

We don't need this mess or the traffic, trash, and noise (and maybe even crime!) it would bring! We already have a perfectly good grocery store here in town and don't need a new one. The current store is owned by a well-known local family which does a lot of good in the community—why would we intentionally create competition for them and threaten their business and the jobs of local residents?

The project would also result in cutting down some

beautiful trees and paving over a 25 acre area which is currently a beautiful woodsy oasis in our bucolic countryside. The neighbors don't want this project and almost unanimously believe it will be of no benefit to the town. We urge the members of the Planning and Zoning Commission to vote "NO" and we ask the Town Mayor and Council to use their influence with the Commission to defeat this proposal. After all, the Council appointed the PZC members and thus have the right to voice their opinions on this issue and thus protect the Town.

And we'd remind the Mayor and Council that Fall elections are not far away and town residents will have a LONG memory when it comes to deciding who we'll vote to re-elect ....OR NOT!!

Sincerely,
Marcia Richards and the 50+ members of SWAT-"Save What's Already There"

Anybody Home? Vote YES

Hello, anybody home? We finally have a chance to increase our tax base and finally bring new revenue to our town. Our taxes are way too high, spending is out of control as it is. This proposal is a no brainer. Vote YES!

Russ Spinasky

Golden Opportunity

Pilgrim Enterprises is offering our town a golden opportunity: cleaning up a dumpy looking area, new tax revenue, employment. All the things our town needs to move into the 21st century. Our Chamber of Commerce and Economic Development Commission have strongly endorsed this project. Now it's up to our Planning and Zoning Commission.

Terri Chambers

Smell the Coffee

New stores, a new restaurant, jobs, a cleaning up of an

overgrown dead zone area-what is there not to like? The PZC members all live in Covingford, they must see the benefits of this proposal. Let's go guys and gals, smell the coffee!

Joe Schlobonick

Where Does It Stop?

Covingford is faced with a proposal that will change it forever—we will never recover. The destruction of an open space area, heavy traffic, more pavement, strangers, loss of our small town atmosphere - it goes on and on. Where does it stop?

Val Novak

Get Out of Our Town

Who are these developers? Pilgrim Enterprises? What do we know about them? Just a bunch of out-of-towners looking to make a quick buck in Covingford, and then they will leave our bucolic community. Time to put our foot down and just say "get out of our Town."

Ernie Lombardo

Loss of Our Way of Life

Covingford will never be the same. The proposed shopping center will change our way of life forever, no going back. Our quiet residential New England town will become a paved over community, just another over-developed suburb, like so many others. Let's stop this nonsense. NOW!

Dolores Gentile

Chapter 19
SPECIAL COUNCIL MEETING

Thursday, March 21

"I am now calling this special meeting to order. Since this is a special meeting with only one item on the agenda, an executive session on personnel, there will be no public input or discussion. The Council will go into executive session pursuant to the State's sunshine laws, which allow us to do this, although any votes taken have to be done in open session, and therefore . . ."

"Excuse me Mr. Mayor," interrupted Janet Johnson. "The public needs to know what this personnel session is all about. The public has a right to know," she persisted. All eyes in the room focused on her.

The Council Chambers went quiet, amplifying the loud ticking of the clock. The few citizens present, the faithful few that closely followed the Council meeting, turned back to focus on the Mayor to see his response. They knew that an executive session just on personnel was unusual, very unusual. The little old lady in the front row abruptly stopped her knitting,

"I'm sorry Janet. The statutes allow us to go into executive session without identifying what or whom the personnel session is about. The only ones in the session will be Council members and the Town Manager. I will now entertain a motion to go into executive session and request everyone to leave the room as soon as we vote to go into the private session."

The motion passed. The atmosphere in the room bore a close resemblance to a wake as people slowly filtered out of the Council Chambers.

"What the hell are they up to now?" asked one resident as they exited the town hall into the blustery March evening. Despite the temperatures finally climbing above freezing, the strong winds made the chill factor very uncomfortable.

"They always seem to be hiding things, damn politicians. Can't trust them," replied another as he pulled up the collar of his coat against the brisk March wind.

Janet said nothing, but scribbled a few notes, holding onto her notepad to stop the papers from blowing away. Even she was puzzled at the odd behavior of the Council. Something was up, and it probably wasn't good.

Council Holds Personnel Executive Session
Mayor refuses to Disclose Why
By Janet Johnson
Inquirer Staff Reporter
March 22

The Covingford Town Council held an unusual Special Council meeting on personnel last night. Citing State Statutes, Mayor Powers refused to disclose what the meeting was about or who the personnel issue involved. Despite a protest from this reporter, the Mayor continued to refuse to elaborate. The legal notice of the meeting that was posted in the Town Clerk's office only stated "Special Town Council Meeting, Council Chambers, Executive Session-Personnel March 21, 7:00pm."

Although the Council met the letter of the law, the special meeting was highly unusual. After the public was forced to leave the room, several residents in attendance had things to say. "Damn unusual, what the hell are they hiding now?" observed Peter Wrang on his way out. Vic Malenchuck expressed similar concerns, "They always seem to be hiding things, damn politicians, can't trust them."

The Council stayed in Executive Session for over two hours. They then adjourned without further action or comment. Although several council members were contacted after the meeting, none of them would comment, either on or off the record. Again, this is very unusual. There is no evidence that the session was in any way related to the major shopping center proposal before the Planning and Zoning Commission.

Although that proposal is in the hands of the PZC, the Town Council did recently receive a fiscal report on it from the Town Manager. The Inquirer has formally requested the report, but to date, has not received a copy. The Mayor has said that the Council will be discussing the report in public at its next regular meeting.

Chapter 20
THE PLANNING AND ZONING COMMISSION VOTE

Monday, March 25

"It now being 7:00 pm, March 25th, I will hereby call this meeting to order. The date, time and place of this meeting have been duly warned in the public newspaper and on-line," announced Jim Bradley as he convened the Planning and Zoning Commission meeting. The room, the Council Chambers in the town hall, was jammed, standing room only, but the mood was different, very different than the hearings held four weeks previously in the high school cafeteria.

Jim looked out at the crowd; memories of the emotionally charged nights of the public hearings struck him. *Almost four weeks ago* he realized. But tonight, he observed, the crowd was smaller, more subdued, almost resigned, all waiting in anticipation of the vote of the Planning and Zoning Commission. An eerie quiet permeated the room. He recognized almost everyone - several Council members including Keith Mitchell who sat right in the front row; Attorney Burns who was sitting with Marcia Richards and many of her SWAT organizers; Attorney Cimione who was with the President and another individual from Pilgrim Enterprises, Peter and Sal; Janet Johnson, and even Mr. and Ms. Ashley who recently had the drainage issue before the Council. He noticed Dom the Bomb waddling his way over to the vacant seat next to Pete and Sal. The Mayor was standing in the back of the room with other Town Council members. *Interesting, I don't see the Town Manager, he hasn't missed a meeting yet,* Bradley thought. *Hmmm, and I don't recognize that sinister looking character standing off by himself. He seems more intent on looking at Dom coming in rather than up here at the Commission. Strange.*

"Following our meeting procedure," Bradley then continued in a loud voice, "this meeting is only for the Commission to discuss and vote; no public input. The vote will be a simple aye or nay vote on the proposed shopping center." He again scanned the room, every eye, except the stranger, stared back at him. No one spoke. He noted that the returning stares were just that, focused stares at the Commission and himself.

"This vote should be interesting," Peter whispered to his cousin Sal. "I think we're ok, I think we got the votes. Dom assured me again yesterday he had weaved his magic."

"Black magic is more like it," Sal responded.

"I still don't know how the chairman or Commissioner Erickson will vote, she's so damn independent. But, whatever, we definitely got two votes, and Dom assured me he lined up the third vote. Our people certainly came through on those letters to the editor and the lawn signs. Certainly pays to have people that want to keep you happy," Peter snickered. "Remind me to send them a personal Christmas card next year."

"Will do, yeah, it does help to have contacts, that's for sure," replied Sal. "And that phone call made to Wiggins certainly helped to remind him on how his brother-in-law got his job in public works. He said he had already spoken to Dom, no resistance. He insisted he was voting in favor of the project even before my call. He knows what is best for the town. Courtney also indicated that he was strongly in favor, has been right along, although he did not appreciate the call from Dom. So that gives us the two definite votes."

"And we definitely got the third," interrupted Dom in an out-of-breath whisper as he quickly took his seat, a big grin on his face. "I didn't get a chance to update you, but I spoke with Jerry Katz again just this morning, and reminded him of a little driving incident about a year and a half ago when he had consumed a few too many drinks. I had spoken with him a few days ago and refreshed his memory of our little chat last summer at the political picnic, and boy, that was a picnic," Dom smiled at his mental flashback of his encounter with Katz. "Jerry certainly had been very surprised I even knew about his driving and drinking incident. You should have seen his face," Dominic grinned. "So, gentlemen, I think we are all set. That should give us at least the third vote we need," Dominic gloated with a satisfied smirk on his face.

"Super, Dom, you did good," Peter commented. "Looks like things will work out after all. So much riding on this vote, and as long as we get three votes, we're home free. Anything over three's a bonus. I don't know how Bradley will vote, he has kept his cards close to the vest, but you never know. But all we need is the three, just three out of the five," he said very slowly, "and maybe we'll get four, or even a grand slam of all five!"

"There being a full commission of all five members," Bradley voice interrupted their conversation, "Does any Commission member wish to discuss the proposal anymore?"

Silence, just a slight shaking of heads.

"Hearing no request for more discussion," Bradley continued with a slight hint of relief in his voice. "I will call for a vote after there is a motion on the floor. Would someone like to make a motion to . . .

"Mr. Chairman," interrupted Katz in a very nervous tone.' Excuse me, I. . . I, I have to say something that will. . ."

"I will call for a full discussion once there is a motion and second on the floor," Bradley interrupted in an irritated tone.

"I'm sorry Mr. Chair, but I must say something, NOW," Katz said in a stronger voice.

Bradley hesitated, then said in a disgusted tone, "Ok, Ok, Jerry, go ahead."

Every eye in the room, including the stranger, suddenly focused on Katz.

"I have spent a great deal of time on this issue and studied all the facts, but, but," Katz hesitated as though trying to build up his courage, "I find I must inform the Commission that I, I . . . will not be voting. I am resigning from the Commission, and here's my official letter of resignation, effective immediately."

The room went absolutely silent. The Commissioners just stared at Katz. Bradley was stunned, speechless. The audience just sat, immobilized, trying to digest the bomb that had just been dropped.

Bradley slowly took the letter from Katz. Not sure of what to do.

Dominic, Peter and Sal sat frozen in place, their mouths wide open. "What the fuck?" whispered Sal.

Bradley, regaining his composure, then announced, "I, I will read this letter for everyone to hear, including the Commission, and" he added slowly "myself."

Dear Chairman Bradley:

The last five weeks have been incredibly intense for me and I have felt the strain. The hearings, news articles, letters to the editor, lawn signs, phone calls, even just trying to shop in town, the deluge of comments and criticism has been constant. After a lengthy conversation with my son, and after consultation with my physician, both are in agreement that it is best if I resign immediately from this volunteer position. My health, both physical and mental, is my first priority. The death of my wife almost a year ago continues to afflict me, and the pressure from this project is too much.

Thus, it is with deep regret that I am submitting my resignation from the Planning and Zoning Commission, effective immediately.

I want to thank the Commission members and especially you, Mr. Chairman, for all the support and consideration that has been extended to me. Service as a Commissioner, albeit for only two years, has been an incredible experience for me. I never fully appreciated the amount of time and effort that volunteers on town boards and commissions put in for the benefit of the town.

I wish the Commission well in its endeavors, especially in its upcoming decision on the shopping center. Thank you.

Sincerely,
Jerry Katz
Cc: Mayor, Town Clerk

The clock on the wall ticked off several seconds, everyone heard it. Then Jerry slowly and silently stood, picked up his coat, and left the room, a slump in his shoulders.

The room continued in its ghastly quiet state. No one spoke. The letter, so unexpected, caught everyone of guard. The Commission members stared at each other, stunned, their thoughts trying to make sense of the strange turn of events. Their minds, horror struck, grappled as to what this meant for the pending vote.

"What the fuck?" again exclaimed Sal. "What's going on?" The Garganos looked at each other and then at the Bomb, who sat there with his mouth still agape. Dom was in a state of shock. He had just spoken with Katz a few hours previously; there had been no indication of this, no hint, nothing, notta. He had left Katz, convinced that he would vote in favor. *Resignation! Where the hell did that come from?* Dom rubbed his forehead, trying to alleviate the immense headache that had suddenly started. *He can't do this! Who the hell does he think he is?* His concentration was so intense he failed to notice the ominous smile on the stranger who just continued to stare at him.

Janet Johnson had stopped writing, frozen by the news. "Wow", she said, "wow, wow, wow," and scribbled the same words. For the second time in as many weeks, the little old lady, again in the front row, stopped her knitting.

Following a few seconds, Chairman Bradley said slowly, "We wish Jerry all the best in the world, and we will miss him." Still no one spoke. Continuing on, Bradley then announced, "The agenda for tonight was advertised for action by the Commission on the proposed shopping center. So, we will continue with the posted agenda and have the vote. However, in light of this resignation, there are now only four voting members on the Commission. We still have a quorum. To approve of the application, three of the four members present must approve of the project, the same number as before. However, if a majority of the Commission votes against the project, or, if it is split 2-2 on the vote, the application fails since it will not meet the necessary majority vote requirement. Do the Commission members understand this?"

The members, still in shock at Katz's resignation, all nodded their head in agreement. A slight murmur spread through the audience.

"We have had considerable discussion on this issue, and we all sat through three nights of hearings listening to all sides. Everyone has had the opportunity to make their arguments and counter-arguments known. We have a complete application before us. So, I will proceed to ask for a motion on the Pilgrim Enterprises shopping center application," Bradley said as he scanned the Commission members.

The members all sat quietly, not wanting to prolong the dreaded vote before them. Either way they knew they would be subject to severe criticism. The letters to the editor, the lawn signs, the hearings, the intensity of this proposal had taken on herculean proportions. None of them had any delusions as to what the vote would mean for them going forward. They lived in this community, went to school here, raised their families here, attended social functions and had many friends, although the later might diminish after their vote, whatever it was. Never had the members, nor the town, seen such an issue that had become so emotional and so divided the community. It was a no-win alternative. Several of them were suddenly secretly envious of Katz for his last minute decision to back out. If it had even entered their minds, a few of them might have also considered it, but that time had passed.

"I will now call for a vote on the proposal, and if the clerk would please record all votes by name. To start the vote, I need a motion and a second on the floor. Do I hear a motion?"

"I move to approve of the zone change for the shopping center as requested by Pilgrim Associates," offered Commissioner Courtney. No one spoke, the room remained still.

"I, I second the motion," Commissioner Wiggins, sheepishly added, thoughts of his brother-in-law flashed in his mind.

"I have a motion to approve the zone change by Commissioner Courtney, seconded by Commissioner Wiggins," announced Chairman Bradley. "Is there any further discussion on the motion?" He looked around the table as the remaining three members stared back at him. No one said a word.

"There being no further discussion, all in favor please say aye and also raise your hand."

Two hands went up simultaneously with two ayes.

"All against?" Bradley asked. One hand went up, that of Marilyn Erickson, who also exclaimed "Nay "in a loud clear voice. All eyes in the room suddenly focused on the Chairman. Everyone did the simple math. Bradley's vote was the deciding vote; it would be either 3-1 in favor or a tie at 2-2. Eternity measured in seconds.

Bradley slowly raised his hand and simply announced, "I vote no." More silence.

"As chairman, I hereby declare that the zone change petition fails on a 2-2 vote. It is a tie; there is no approval. No majority vote; the petition of Pilgrim Associates has failed to receive approval."

The silence grew louder!

"I want to thank the Commission members for their intensive work on this proposal. Your efforts and diligence are appreciated," Bradley said, and then announced, "Motion to adjourn? " Motion was made and seconded, and the vote passed unanimously. This meeting is adjourned," announced the Chairman."

The audience broke out in applause. Members of the SWAT team were ecstatic, hugging one another, tears flowing down their cheeks. Attorney Burns was almost lifted up and carried around the room! The little old lady just nodded, a broad smile crossed her face, and she resumed her knitting. Councilor Mitchell sat stunned, not believing his ears; his mouth moved but nothing came out. The Garganos turned and stormed out of the room not saying a word although several people present would later insist they heard a litany of foul words and threats from them. Louie the Enforcer looked over at the President of Pilgrim Enterprises, and received an almost imperceptible nod from him.

Dominic the "Bomb" sat frozen in place; his face white with fear. His confidence in his recent maneuvers that he had arranged so carefully to insure Katz's vote had disappeared in the stroke of a pen. He had not seen this coming. He had just spoken to Katz a few hours ago. Dom had assured everyone, including Louie the "Enforcer," that he had taken care of things. He started to shake, all 300 pounds bringing his wooden chair to the edge of collapse. He continued to wiggle his head in disbelief, totally unaware of the sinister character making his way towards him.

KATZ'S' SURPRISE RESIGNATION STUNS TOWN-
RESIGNATION IMPACTS SHOPPING CENTER PROPOSAL
WHICH FAILS ON A 2-2 TIE VOTE
March 26
By Janet Johnson
Inquirer Staff Reporter

Covingford: Members of the Planning and Zoning Commission and the public were stunned at last night's PZC meeting when Commissioner Jerry Katz suddenly announced he was resigning effective immediately (before the critical vote), citing health concerns. His unanticipated announcement was greeted with absolute silence as people struggled to digest its implications.

Chairman Jim Bradley, also caught off guard, immediately announced that three votes were still required to pass the zoning request from Pilgrim Enterprises for the shopping center, but that since only four members were left on the commission, a tie vote of 2-2 would not result in its approval.

Commissioner Courtney made a motion to approve; it was seconded by Commissioner Wiggins. In the vote that followed, Courtney and Wiggins voted in favor, Commissioner Erickson voted against. Chairman Bradley then voted against, resulting in a 2-2 tie. Thus, the motion failed to receive the required 3 votes for approval.

The resignation of Jerry Katz created the tie vote. If Katz had remained on the Commission and resigned right after the meeting instead of before the vote, the outcome could have been quite different. One way or the other, the vote would have been 3-2. People interviewed after the meeting indicated nobody was sure which way Katz would have voted, but there were indications he was leaning in favor of the project but for some reason, still had serious reservations.

Pilgrim Enterprises' Attorney Cimione indicated that his clients would not spend any more money or time on the project and were pulling out. Cimione also reiterated to this reporter a cryptic remark he made at the last night of the PZC public hearings, "Now let's see what is going to go in there on that site." He would not elaborate.

Mayor Powers said that the Council would move immediately to fill Katz's seat, and the person appointed would only serve for the remaining term of Katz, which will be up this November. Town Manager Kurt Thomas was not available for comment.

EPILOGUE

COVINGFORD TOWN MANAGER UNEXPECTEDLY RESIGNS-TOWN OFFICIALS MUM ON REASONS
April 16
By Janet Johnson
Inquirer Staff Reporter

Covingford. Town Manager Kurt Thomas unexpectedly submitted a letter of resignation to the Town Council last night, effective June 30, the last day of the Town's fiscal year. His letter was read at the start of last night's regular Council meeting. No specific reason was stated in the Manager's letter other than it was "time to move on."

Mayor Powers announced that "by mutual agreement" the Town Manager was leaving and the Mayor expressed his "regret" over the resignation and wished the Town Manager well. He said the Council would start immediately on a search for a new Manager, but the process could take four months or longer. An interim manager will be appointed in the meantime. He declined further comment on the actual resignation. There were no other comments by the Councilors at the meeting, and the Mayor moved the meeting to the next agenda item.

Shortly thereafter the Council meeting was adjourned without further comment by the Mayor or the Council members. Attempts by this reporter for further clarification were futile.

COVINGFORD TOWN MANAGER'S RESIGNATION A SHOCK TO MANY RESIDENTS
April 18
SPECIAL INVESTIGATIVE REPORT
By Janet Johnson
Inquirer Staff Reporter

———

Covingford. Town Manager Kurt Thomas' unexpected resignation three days ago to the Town Council caught numerous people off guard. His resignation is effective June 30th, the last day of the town's fiscal year. Numerous people active in Covingford's local government who were contacted said they had no indication the resignation was coming. Research by this reporter in the last several days has revealed that several events were linked.

As background, on March 21st the Covingford Town Council held a special executive session meeting whose sole purpose was a "personnel issue" according to the public notice that was filed. This reporter and the general public in attendance were required to leave the meeting room since the Executive Session was limited to Council members and the Town Manager.

Mayor Powers stated at that time that "if any votes were taken, they would have to be done in open session." According to the official minutes of the meeting, no votes were taken although the meeting lasted over two hours.

According to an unnamed reliable source, Town Manager Thomas had been directed to prepare for the Town Council an analysis of the financial aspects of the proposed shopping center plan before the Planning and Zoning Commission and "its impact on the Town." According to the source, although the Town Manager did as directed in mid-March, he also included information on issues he felt important regarding "the impact on the Town" that were not directly related to financial issues. This information addressed other elements such as environmental issues and the impact of the development on the nearby neighborhood, which had been fighting the proposal. Some Council members apparently were not happy that the Town Manager's fiscal report submitted to the Town Council "went beyond" what the Council was looking for.

The source explained that one Councilor (un-named) was "outraged" that the Town Manager had "exceeded his authority" by including in the report "extraneous, erroneous, misleading, and irrelevant information on the impact on the neighborhood." The meeting became quite can-tankerous and heated, split along party lines.

The PZC on March 25, on a 2-2 tie vote, (one Commissioner had unexpectedly resigned right before the vote), failed to approve the proposed shopping center, effectively killing the project. Pilgrim Enterprises, the developers, subsequently stated that they are abandoning the project and will be looking at developing in other "more friendly" communities. The shopping center has been very controversial in town, with neighbor-hood protests and almost daily letters to the edi-tor, both in favor and against. The proposal would have generated between $1.5 and $2 million dol-lars in additional tax revenue to Covingford, along with many new job opportunities. The adjacent neighborhood had come out in strong opposition to the plan, stating it would devastate their way of life. They even hired an attorney to represent them at the hearing.

This reporter's source, confirmed by others, also stated that there were other items that some of the councilors were not happy with, such as com-munications with the Council and the fact that the Town Manager's budget proposal required a significant tax increase. Several Council members had wanted the Town Manager's budget to have a "zero" budget increase, despite a decrease in State revenue to the Town as well as new labor contracts that the Council itself recently ratified. According to the public record, there never was a formal vote of the Town Council on this budget directive. However, tax increases are normally avoided in the local election years, which Covingford is facing this November.

Interestingly, the Town Manager, in an interview with this reporter a few months ago, had observed that "your friends come and go, but your enemies accumulate." Apparently, at that time, he was picking up vibes of dissatisfaction with some Council members. Neither the Mayor nor the Council members have made any public comment on the resignation, citing it as a "personnel" issue.

Kurt Thomas has been Town Manager in Covingford for over ten years; he is the longest serving Town Manager. When contacted directly, Thomas just commented that "he was exploring other options and already had a few irons in the fire." At this point it is unknown what specific plans he may have for the future, but public sentiment expressed to this reporter indicates he will be sorely missed.

Additional efforts were made to obtain comments by Mayor Powers and Manager Thomas but both declined public comment. The unnamed source did indicate that the severance package for the Manager, still being worked out, requires that he not comment on his resignation nor on the Town Council. Councilor Mitchell, a regular critic of the Manager, was also asked for reaction to the comments stated above by the unnamed source, and if he had any comments prior to this reporter going to press. He loudly declined and abruptly hung up on this reporter.

EIGHT MONTHS LATER – DECEMBER

TOWN COUNCIL: In the subsequent November election, Covingford's minority party became the majority party. This was due to a vigorous political campaign by newcomer Chris Clark, the irate citizen who was angry with the Council for denial of his sewer connection earlier in the year. Clark secured a seat on the Town Council. Councilor Kathleen Corey was the high vote getter, and, based on her Council experience and because her party was now the majority party due to Clark being elected, was selected as the Mayor of Covingford. Councilor Mitchell became the minority leader since his party no longer has the majority on the Council. Former Mayor Powers had decided not to run again, and his seat was lost to newcomer Chris Clark.

TOWN MANAGER: Kurt Thomas secured another town manager position in a larger community west of Hartford. As Kurt had commented to Janet in her article on his resignation, "Your friends come and go, but your enemies accumulate. It's time to leave." Per the town charter requirement of his new community, Kurt had to establish residence, and, inasmuch as Covingford was only 45 minutes away, he was able to commute while he placed his Covingford condo on the market. His real estate agent assured him it would be sold by the start of the Spring. Kurt kept in touch with many of his friends from Covingford, and closely followed the local news articles by Janet Johnson.

THE GARGANOS: Peter and Sal, clearly dissatisfied with the vote by the Zoning Commission, were active in the nomination process for candidates from their party to run for the Town Council. They were vehement in their positions that the candidates clearly understood the need to promote economic development in the town, and the importance of appointing the "right" people to the Planning and Zoning Commission.

PLANNING AND ZONING COMMISSION: The vacant PZC seat that had been held by Commissioner Katz was filled temporarily by the Town Council. The temporary member was clear that he would serve only until November, and did not want to be re-appointed after the elections, citing the heavy time demand required to be on the Commission. The existing members of the various boards and commissions retained their seats until re-appointed or until a new member was appointed to replace them. The new political majority on the Town Council had indicated they intended to maintain the current members of their party on the Commission, especially Jim Bradley, the chairman. The Council majority assured the minority members of the Council they would certainly "listen" to them regarding whom they wanted to appoint to the town boards and commissions, especially the Zoning Commission. The Commission was, after all, "an extremely important commission" in Covingford, and one, in effect, that "controlled the future land use" in the community.

"THE BOMB": Dom the "Bomb" ran into a string of bad luck. In mid-April he was involved in the receiving end of a hit-and-run driver, and spent over five weeks in the hospital. The doctors advised him that he had to lose a substantial amount of weight inasmuch as he would be on crutches for another 6 months and his inactivity made him a prime candidate for a heart attack. In addition to his loss of time and income from work, an attachment was made on his house and it was in danger of foreclosure for non-payment of creditors' bills. Dominic was forced to resign his volunteer position as the party chairman which he was heard to lament, "hurt him more than the looming foreclosure of his house." Snowball moped around the house while Dominic was in the hospital, clearly missing his master. Dom's wife started a new full time position in a Hartford retail store, quite distressed she was no longer "Queen Bee" in Covingford's politics.

"THE ENFORCER": Louie disappeared from the local scene although there were unconfirmed stories of his whereabouts in the vicinity of Atlantic City.

NEWSPAPER REPORTER: Janet Johnson continued to write for the Inquirer, although on a very limited basis. Her promotion to Assistant Editor gave her several more responsibilities, especially since the Inquirer's circulation had increased dramatically due to the extensive local coverage of the proposed development in Covingford. Her new position involved reviewing government articles on several towns by the Inquirer's local reporters; she also sat on the paper's editorial staff. The word on the street was that she had a knowledgeable confidant she could turn to, a confidant not only very familiar with Covingford but a person who was an expert in local government. This unnamed source had numerous meetings with her, and was advising her on a regular basis, a very regular basis.

THE SITE: Based on an anonymous call, the shopping center proposal brought the fallow land onto the radar screen of both the local and State officials. The State department responsible for environmental protection, in conjunction with the town, started a series of tests on the property, including several random test borings. Preliminary results indicated high levels of underground contamination, although the contamination was very spotty and could easily have been overlooked in the earlier random environmental testing. However, the findings resulted in the scheduling of numerous more test borings for the following spring after the ground thawed from the early Connecticut ground freeze. In the meantime, the Trust controlling the site was exploring low income housing which would allow it to bypass certain local zoning regulations.

LITTLE OLD LADY: The little old lady finished her knitting for two of her grandchildren, and started knitting for another grandchild on the way. "After all," she was recently quoted in the newspaper, "I never realized how interesting local government is, and now that I attend all of the Council meetings, I will have lots of time to knit while I keep my eye on those rascals. And," she added with a smirk and a wink, "I may even run for the Town Council!"

AUTHOR'S NOTE

Local government is not a spectator sport. Throughout the country, people associate with their local government. This is especially true in New England, as witnessed in the fictional town of Covingford. Residents get involved in their town affairs, and many serve as volunteers on the boards and commissions. Often they just change from one board to another, but continually stay involved in town affairs. Local politics becomes a way of life for many, and in some cases, even forms their social circles. They take local government seriously, very seriously. The Town Meeting and other local public meetings are alive and well in New England. It is not uncommon to have hundreds of people show up to vote on the annual budget or on a hot topic in town.

Interestingly, towns and cities are not mentioned in the US Constitution. The creation of the towns (and townships) and cities is left up to each State. States decide how much power and authority each municipality will have. They exist and only have the power expressly granted to them by the state; this is known as the Dillon Rule, dating back Judge Dillon in 1872. Thus, States have the right to intervene and even take over operations of the city or town, such as what took place in Detroit when it recently ran into serious financial difficulty.

Several states have a concept known as "Home Rule," where the States grant authority for towns and cities to self-govern. They decide on their own form of government and how they will operate. Home Rule varies by state, with some communities exercising more independence from the State than others. Most states have county government, where various government services are performed at the county level. Only two states, Connecticut and Rhode Island, do not have county government, although they have counties.

Local elections in New England occur every other year in the odd year. The even-year elections are reserved for State and federal offices. Historically, New Englanders don't trust "the rascals" in local office, and want the ability to throw them out every two years if needed.

The New England states vary somewhat in the forms of local government, but they are variations of several basic forms: Town Meeting/Selectmen, Town Meeting/Selectmen/Manager, Council/Manager, and Council/Mayor.

In several states, there are also chief administrative officers and administrative assistants to assist in running the day-to-day operations in local government. Interestingly, Maine has a unique form called Plantations, used in small rural areas. Some Town Council/Town Manager forms retain the town meeting. In Vermont the words townships, villages and select boards are used.

Connecticut has three basic forms of local government:

- Selectman/Town Meeting
- Mayor/Council
- Town Council/Town Manager.

There are several variations within these three forms, including a representative Town Meeting where an elected body replaces the town meeting.

Maine has five common forms:

- Town Meeting -Selectmen
- Town Meeting-Selectmen-Manager
- Town Meeting-Council-Manager
- Council/Manager
- Mayor/Council

In Connecticut, the form of government is decided by State Statutes which allow local governments to operate directly under the Statutes or adopt their own charter or "constitution". If they choose the latter option, they can elect the form of government they wish to have. The decision is then made by a referendum.

Local government is extensive in New England. The term municipality is used in describing towns and cities. Connecticut, the second smallest state geographically, has 169 towns and cities, each one independent. In neighboring Rhode Island, the smallest state, there are 39 municipalities. New Hampshire has 234 municipalities, Vermont has 246 towns and cities, and Maine has almost 500!

In the Selectmen/Town Meeting form, the First Selectman is the chief executive officer, and usually with the two (or more) other selectmen, comprise the Board of Selectmen. The Board's job is to run the town on a day-to-day basis, with this major responsibility falling to the First Selectman. The Town Meeting adopts the annual town budget, and depending upon the town charter, is convened for other legislative functions.

In the first two forms, the First Selectman or the Mayor is directly elected and serves as the chief executive officer of the municipality, receiving a salary. These elected positions normally have a term of two years, although a few municipalities have extended the term to four years. Many of the three forms may also have a Board of Finance, which, depending upon the charter and the personalities can be very powerful in financial decisions.

In the Mayor/Town Council form, the Mayor is the chief executive officer. He/she runs for and is elected as Mayor. He is not a member of the Town Council. Mayor/Town Council forms are normally found in larger cities, but there is no set rule; it is up to each community to decide what form of government it wants. Depending upon the charter, there can be a "strong Mayor" with substantial administrative duties, or a "weak Mayor" who does not have this authority. For example, a weak Mayor may have to have the Council approve all the appointments by the Mayor of department heads. These "strong" and "weak" titles are also greatly influenced by the personality of the Mayor.

In the Town Council/Town Manager form of government, the Council is elected by the voters to exercise overall control of the local government. The Council then appoints a town manager to serve as the chief executive, who runs the town on a day-to-day basis and carries out the policy direction of the Town Council. There is a chairman of the Council, sometimes called a Mayor. In some towns, this position is elected independently from the Council, and when elected, he/she is then the head of the Town Council and a member of the Council itself. Normally this is an unpaid position. Sometimes the candidate who is not successful in the election of Mayor becomes a member of the Town Council; other times the loser is out altogether. Other variations include scenarios where the high vote getter becomes the chairman of the Council, frequently with the title of Mayor. Sometimes the mayor or Chairman of Town Council is selected directly by the Council itself.

Such was the case in the Town of Covingford. In any case, this position is <u>not</u> the chief executive officer of the town and normally is not paid. The person is a member of the Town Council, runs the Council meetings, is the presiding officer, is viewed as the political head who directs public policy and represents the Town Council at ceremonial functions. The Council may perform all the legislative duties, or they may be restricted by a town meeting or a referendum.

In the Town Council/Town Manager form, as was the case in Covingford, the Town Manager is the chief executive officer of the town. He or she is not elected, but appointed by the Town Council based on professional qualifications such as education and experience. Normally he or he has to move into town after appointment, but this is not always the requirement. The Manager is in charge of handling the day-to-day operations of the community, including the preparation of the annual budget and hiring staff. He or she works directly for the Town Council which sets public policy for the Manager to carry it out.

Towns often adopt the Town Council/Town Manager form of government for several reasons: the desire to have a professional trained in local government to run the day-to-day operations and serve as the chief executive officer as a non-political person. Sometimes, towns just have trouble finding a candidate to run for the First Selectman position. Low pay, long hours, the complexity of the position, lots of aggravation, and a job guarantee of only two years with no unemployment compensation if not re-elected, all add to the problem of finding a qualified person to run for the elected position of chief executive officer.

Normally the Manager does not change with local elections since the position is non-partisan; this provides an element of stability in local government. Managers however, do serve at the pleasure of the Town Councils. Often Managers, after several years in office, find that the people that hired them are no longer on the

Town Council and feel no allegiance to him or her. Sometimes the Councilors want to hire "their own" Manager. Hence the expression in the story "your friends come and go, but your enemies accumulate." When this occurs, it becomes time for the Manager to move on. This is an accepted risk of the profession. If no employment contract exists, a severance package is worked out. Such was the case with Kurt Thomas when the Council indicated it was time for him to move on. Oftentimes it is the Manager who, after several years in the town, chooses to leave the community to seek other opportunities.

According to the National League of Cities (NLC), the Council/Manager form is the most common form of local government. There is also a professional organization of town and city managers, the International City/County Management Association (ICMA), and according to ICMA, the average tenure of a manager in a community is 7.2 years. ICMA is housed in Washington, DC. It maintains and enforces a professional Code of Ethics for managers, and provides extensive support for its members.

ACKNOWLEDGEMENTS

There were several people who greatly assisted me with ideas, comments, and of course the constant editing and proofreading in writing a novel. Although I spoke with numerous people in the development of this story, there are a few individuals who are important to be recognized for their assistance.

My wife, Terri, constantly offered comments and suggestions. As a retired public school reading specialist, her sharp eye in proof reading was none short of amazing. Despite the myriad times I read and re-read the drafts, she picked up improper English, punctuation changes, and offered continual editorial comments.

My friend and neighbor Ray Poet, helped me to finally bring this novel to conclusion, twenty years after I started it. Ray and I spent many hours in discussions on the story line, alternative plot directions, and its surprise ending. Our meetings provided a match of two governmental careers, mine in local and state government and Ray in the federal system. As a retired federal employee whose career involved interpreting and implementing federal regulations, he also provided great support on the logistics of the time sequences in the story line.

Others who assisted in reading drafts and providing significant insights include my daughter Katie Connolly, who used the writing skills she honed when she was on her law school editorial board. Preliminary reviews by fellow practioners include Aaron Chrostowsky, a Town Manager in Maine, and Susan Bransfield, a First Selectwoman in Connecticut. Both of their insights were most helpful since they work daily in the trenches in the administration of local government.

HIDDEN AGENDAS

CAST OF MAJOR CHARACTERS

Kurt Thomas - Town Manager of Covingford.

Dom "The Bomb" Columbo - head of the town political committee.

Sal and Peter Gargano - cousins who are a major force in the political climate of Covingford.

Janet Johnson - reporter for the *Hartford Inquirer* –

Jerry Katz - newest member of the Zoning Commission.

Jim Bradley - Chairman of the local Planning and Zoning Commission (PZC).

Mayor Robert Powers - head of the Town Council.

Councilor Keith Mitchell - powerful member of the Town Council.

Attorney Patricia Burns - represents residents fighting shopping center.

Attorney Richard Cimione - represents Pilgrim Enterprises, the developers

Louie "The Enforcer" - the heavy outside gun whose job is to threaten Dom "The Bomb."